Years before, Saul Mandisa came to Vegas to work on stage . . . only to find out it requires a lot of dancing, and he has two left feet. When his minimum wage job didn't quite cover food and rent, he took a few side hustles that he wasn't proud of. Finally landing steady work allowed him to extricate himself from that life . . . or so Saul thought.

Even after five years, Saul would never forget Reagan the Hammer—right hand and enforcer to the infamous crime boss—Luigi Arnasta. At first, he ignores Reagan's calls. Then he does his best to avoid the man—and his henchmen—at all costs. After all, Saul wants nothing to do with that life, and he never had. His luck runs out when he meets a couple of friends for drinks and discovers one of them essentially sold him out.

To Saul's shock, a sexy Frenchman steps in and sends Reagan packing—a man named Jean-Paul Tremblay. When Saul discovers his savior is a vampire who seems to think he's the other half of Jean-Paul's soul, will he risk taking a chance on the devil he doesn't know?

Enchanted by a Vampire
Copyright © 2022 Charlie Richards
ISBN: 978-1-4874-3696-4
Cover art by Angela Waters

Published by eXtasy Books Inc

Look for us online at:
www.eXtasybooks.com

ENCHANTED BY A VAMPIRE
A LOVING NIP 29

BY

CHARLIE RICHARDS

DEDICATION

Quand le vin est tiré, il faut le boire. — Once the first step is taken, there's no going back.
~French Proverb

CHAPTER ONE

Feeling his phone vibrate in his pocket, Saul Mandisa ignored it as he led a pair of customers to their table. He placed their menus in front of each, starting with the woman. After letting them know that their server would be Kyle, Saul wished them a great meal and started back toward the front where he knew more people waited.

Saul took a few quick seconds to pull out his phone. Waking the device, he spotted the text message and grimaced when he saw who it was from—Reagan, no last name. He shoved the phone back into his pocket. Saul didn't need to know Reagan's last name. He knew the sender.

Reagan the Hammer.

A chill worked its way up Saul's spine, even in the heat of the casino restaurant. He did his best to ignore it as he returned to work. Saul had another hour to his shift, after all.

Then I need to figure out another variation to my way home.

On autopilot, Saul greeted the next group—a trio of women. He absently recognized the flirting of the brunette as she touched his arm. On reflex, Saul flexed his bicep before easing to the left and urging her and her friends to follow him.

While Saul could acknowledge the woman was beautiful, he wouldn't bother pursuing her interest for a couple of reasons.

First of all, he never picked up dates—or tricks—where he worked. If things didn't work out, the person would know where he worked, could bother him there, and things could end up awkward. Saul would never jeopardize his job by act-ing so foolishly. It had taken him years to get his position as host and waiter at *Emeril's*, and with tips, as long as he lived fairly frugally, he made a pretty comfortable living.

Besides, between working out and the occasional night out with friends, Saul really didn't need much.

The second reason was common sense. Having someone in Saul's life meant there would be someone Reagan could use against him. When dealing with the seedy parts of society, ro-mantic relationships were a liability.

Probably a little cynical, but Saul knew it to be true. He'd seen it happen. Never had he been happier to land a job that allowed him to pull himself out of that life. Saul had never wanted to be a part of it, anyway, but desperate times had called for desperate measures.

Had to find a way to eat.

And now, after nearly five years, Reagan's coming round again. Why couldn't he just leave me alone?

Saul knew the answer, however. If they were coming to him, it was because they wanted him to drive for them. Years before, he'd used skills learned racing his buddies on dirt roads back in Hicksville, and he'd been a wheelman for the crime boss, Luigi Arnasta.

He'd counted himself lucky that the guy had seemed to for-get he existed. Of course, him moving to a new place probably helped. Between a new home not in Luigi's territory, plus a job clear of it, too, he'd successfully slipped off Luigi's radar.

Until now.

Pushing thoughts of his problems to the back of his mind, Saul returned his focus to finishing out his shift.

"You doin' anything fun tonight, man?"

Saul glanced toward Billy, a bus boy whose shift had also just ended. Offering the friendly and young—Saul figured Billy couldn't have been more than nineteen—man a small smile, he lifted one shoulder in a shrug. "Working out," he hedged. Lifting his right arm, he flexed his impressive bicep. "These babies don't stay pumped on their own."

Billy's eyes widened as he stared at Saul's arm. His cheeks took on a hint of pink, and he glanced away. He even swallowed hard enough for his Adam's apple to bob.

Quickly lowering his arm, Saul did his best to ignore the young man's obvious attraction.

Yeah, he has needy bottom boy written all over him. So not my type.

On the occasion that Saul took a man home, he chose someone robust enough to go all night . . . and who could switch it up. Saul enjoyed bottoming just as much as topping. The feel of a hard cock stretching him, of a man's thick meat sliding over his prostate, was just as tantalizing as feeling the squeeze and heat of a body wrapped around his erection.

Hmmm . . . maybe I'll pick up a guy to have some fun with this evening. I don't have to work tomorrow.

Plus, Saul was meeting a couple of friends for drinks at a wine bar that evening. The place wasn't his usual haunt, but he didn't mind. He knew there would be next to no chance that Reagan or his goons would happen to drop by a place like that, either.

"Well." Saul slapped Billy on the upper arm lightly, making certain to moderate his strength. After all, it looked like a stiff wind could knock over the young, slender guy. Doing his best to try to move past the awkward moment, Saul added, "Have a great night, man."

Without waiting for a response, Saul opened the door and hustled out of the room. He turned left and took a side hall. While the exit he chose wasn't the closest to his route home, he hadn't used it in a while.

Plus, the prior day, when Saul had intended to use that door, he'd spotted Dario leaning against a nearby building. The man had tried to disguise himself by wearing a ballcap, but it had been an epic fail. Saul would be able to recognize the hulking man's broad shoulders anywhere.

Saul had been able to slip back into the casino, choosing another way to get home.

God, how long am I going to have to dodge these guys?

However long it takes.

While Saul occasionally mentally toyed with the idea of moving to a new city, he truly loved living in Las Vegas. It didn't matter that he didn't always have a lot of spending money. There were enough free shows that were constantly changing to keep him occupied when he was out of cash.

Saul eased his hoodie onto his head before opening the door. After a discreet glance around and not seeing anyone he recognized, he headed out the door. The warm desert air wrapped around him, and he immediately regretted needing the hoodie.

Oh well. I won't need it long.

Striding swiftly, Saul rounded the building and merged into the flow of pedestrians. He took advantage of the many people around him and lowered the hood. After a glance over his shoulder to confirm he didn't see anyone following him, he removed the hoodie and placed it over his crooked arm.

As much as Saul hoped he was just being paranoid, he feared he wasn't. He spotted a car he recognized and quickly slipped to the right and shortened his stride. Using a large, heavyset man as cover, Saul watched the *El Camino* with black spinning rims creep down the street.

While the slow progress was due in part to the fact that traffic was always extremely heavy on the Las Vegas strip, Saul also made out the goateed features of Gally. The black man scowled, making the scar bisecting his right cheek even more pronounced before it disappeared underneath his facial hair. Saul had heard a few different stories about how Gally had gotten the mark, but he would never try to confirm any of them.

Once Saul could barely make out the vehicle's tail lights in the distance, he let out a low sigh of relief. He crossed the street to the left and headed into the parking garage he had an employee pass for. Saul spotted Daniel leaning against his car, already waiting for him. His buddy owned the vehicle, and in return for a ride, Saul paid for the parking pass.

Fortunately, most of the time, his and Daniel's shifts lined up. It helped that the man was a manager with seniority at the restaurant where he worked, so he could cherry-pick his schedule. He'd worked for Daniel at that same restaurant for almost six months, part-time, before landing the job at *Emeril's* and quitting.

Daniel had then offered to rent him one of his spare bedrooms. At first, Saul had worried that the man saw him as a charity case. As much as he'd really wanted to accept, he'd started to beg off due to his pride. Then Daniel had explained that caring for his mother until she'd passed from leukemia had wiped out his savings and the bit of extra monthly income, along with splitting the expenses and groceries, would be doing him a huge solid.

Saul hadn't been able to say no.

On top of the fantastic new living and commuting arrangements, Saul had helped Daniel set up a really nice home gym in his third bedroom.

"Hey, Saul," Daniel offered, pushing away from the driver's side door. "Everything go okay?"

Nodding, Saul reached for the passenger side door handle. "Yeah." He knew what Daniel was really asking, so as he slipped inside, he admitted, "I spotted Gally on my way here, but he didn't see me."

Daniel had known what Saul was running away from when he'd first moved in. As he started the car, he shook his head. "Damn, buddy. What the hell did Reagan ask for after all this time?"

Saul sighed deeply and shrugged. "I hung up on him and have been doing my best to avoid him ever since."

"That's not gonna work forever," Daniel warned with a grimace as he started driving.

"I know," Saul muttered, scowling out the window.

"Sorry," Daniel murmured in commiseration. After clearing his throat, the older man asked, "So, uh . . . what are you going to do?"

Threading his fingers into his thick blond hair, Saul used the move to tug out his hair band and scratch his scalp at the same time.

"I don't know," Saul admitted softly with a frown.

Saul entered the wine bar and paused in the foyer. Sweeping his attention over the room, he spotted his friends at a tall round table to the right. He bit back a smirk upon seeing Marty already flirting with the woman who appeared to be serving their drinks.

Heading that way, Saul noticed a third drink and settled in the seat before it. "Hey, guys," he greeted, resting his left hand on the table. As Saul exchanged a fist bump with Marty, he asked, "How's it goin'?"

"Good, good," Marty replied. After bumping Saul's fist, he pointed at the glass of wine before him. "I ordered us both a shiraz. Tell me what you think."

"Thanks," Saul replied. To his surprise, when he lifted his fist toward Lawrence, his dark-haired friend just stared at him with worry filling his brown eyes. Lowering his hand to the table, Saul wrapped his fingers around the stemware and cocked his head. "What's wrong, Lawrence?"

Lawrence pushed his wine glass toward the center of the table as he murmured, "I'm really sorry, Saul."

"For what?" Saul asked, glancing between his friends, but Marty looked just as confused as Saul felt.

"I didn't have a choice," Lawrence continued, confusing Saul further. "My sister's hospital bills are killing me, and —" Grimacing, Lawrence rose to his feet, again saying, "Sorry."

"Oh, shit," Marty whispered, his dark eyes widening as he stared beyond Saul's shoulder. "You didn't."

"I'm sorry," Lawrence repeated forlornly. Then he headed away from the table.

Saul watched his friend go, turning in his seat. Spotting Lawrence pause next to Reagan and discreetly take a wad of cash, he felt a trickle of cold panic slither down his spine. As his buddy moved on, Saul met Reagan's cold, blue-eyed gaze.

"I don't think slipping out the back is possible," Marty whispered, his voice strained.

"Afraid not," Saul agreed, keeping his voice just as low as he watched Reagan approach, the man's goons flanking him. "You might want to leave, Marty. I wouldn't want you to get involved in this."

"Lawrence involved me," Marty grumbled. "And next time I see him, I'm gonna kick his ass."

Saul silently agreed, but he understood the man's reasons, too. If the situation were reversed, he wondered if he would do anything for family, too.

I just don't happen to have any to worry about.

"Hello, Saul," Reagan greeted, settling onto Lawrence's vacated stool and pulling the man's untouched wine glass toward himself. With a cold smile, he lifted it. "I warned you that I'd find you." Before taking a sip, Reagan added with a distinctive chill in his voice, "It seems you need a reminder about how my boss always gets what he wants."

Even as Saul forced a little moisture into his throat, he still couldn't find his voice as fear prickled his insides.

CHAPTER TWO

Well, this is unexpected . . . and welcome.

Jean-Paul Tremblay found his attention riveted on the big blond human who'd arrived a couple of moments before. The scent of his blood teased his senses, causing his mouth to water and his fangs to ache in a way that nothing had before. Considering Jean-Paul was nearly three hundred years old and the master of his vampire coven in France, that was saying something.

When the acrid tinge of panic and fear soured the stranger's scent, Jean-Paul snapped out of his shock. He quickly scanned the new arrival at the table, taking in his hard features and cold demeanor. The way a pair of goon-like humans in ill-fitting suits stood a few feet back, leaning against the wine bar, told Jean-Paul all he needed to know.

Even if this human isn't my beloved, I'll still send these assholes packing.

In Jean-Paul's opinion, no one should scent of that much fear . . . especially when he'd smelled so wonderful before.

Jean-Paul narrowed his eyes as he rose to his feet. He picked up his glass of wine and took in the group's demeanor once more. The big blond Jean-Paul desperately wanted to taste had his shoulders hunched, his jaw was set, and his brows were furrowed.

Hmmm . . . I much prefer the smile he'd sported when he first came in.

"Master Jean-Paul?" Julian murmured in French, rising next to him. "What is it?"

Jean-Paul barely spared his head enforcer a glance as he responded in the same language, "I need to help the panicked human at that table." He used his chin to indicate the table where the big human sat. "His blood calls to me."

"His blood?" Julian whispered, shock in his tone even as it oozed into his scent. "Truly?"

Finally, Jean-Paul met Julian's gaze squarely. "*Truly.*"

"May the Fates be kind to us," Julian murmured, moving to flank him.

Jean-Paul shouldn't have been surprised. They'd been waiting to meet up with a few other vampires and their be-loveds, enjoying a glass of wine to pass the time. As it was, Jean-Paul appreciated that his friend, Caspian, and his bunny shifter beloved, Casey, had been running behind.

When Jean-Paul had received a text from the vampire dip-lomat, who he'd become friends with over the last several years, telling him that they would be around fifteen minutes late, Jean-Paul had figured that meant they'd become dis-tracted and ended up having a quickie.

May they take a little while longer.

Approaching the table, Jean-Paul saw the malicious-scent-ing human cast a narrow-eyed gaze upon the human who in-terested him. "Come with me quietly, Saul, and I'll leave your little friend alone." He looked over his shoulder at the bruis-ers behind him, then smirked as he glanced at the third hu-man at the table—Saul's friend. "Of course, my boys would be ever-so-happy to have your friend to play with while you and I . . . chat."

It didn't take any stretch of Jean-Paul's rather poor imagi-nation to figure out what kind of *chat* and *play* this asshole was talking about.

"Take care of his goons," Jean-Paul ordered softly.

With a nod, Julian peeled away from him.

Jean-Paul arrived at the table and eased onto the spare seat, drawing two surprised looks and one malicious one. He ignored the latter and focused on Saul. Needing to banish his surprise swiftly if his ruse was to work, Jean-Paul reached over and threaded his fingers through Saul's hair, cupping his neck.

Then Jean-Paul leaned close and pressed a kiss to the human's jaw, enjoying the hint of whiskers against his lips. "Play along, handsome," he whispered into the human's ear. Pulling back, Jean-Paul allowed his French accent to thicken a smidge as he crooned, "I am so sorry I was late. Traffic held me up." Jean-Paul forced a depreciative laugh as he added, "This Vegas traffic still blows my mind."

"Uh, that's okay," Saul replied slowly, obviously trying to catch up. His scent still screamed of worry, and he glanced toward his antagonist once before refocusing on Jean-Paul. "Um, I'm happy to see you again, but . . . it may not be the best time."

Jean-Paul glanced toward the asshole again. "The timing is fine," he assured, narrowing his eyes as he caught the other guy's anger-filled stare. "You were just heading out. Weren't you?"

Jean-Paul barely resisted trancing the male—his vampiric ability to enter a human's mind and manipulate it—but he figured that would be a little hard to explain to Saul's friend. After all, in order to do that, he would need to haze his eyes. If he confirmed that Saul was his beloved, Jean-Paul would explain why his irises occasionally turned red, but he couldn't share that knowledge with one who was not his fated soul mate.

"The only way I'm leaving is if Saul comes with me," the human declared with a curl of his lip. "The pair of you are welcome, too." He eased the left side of his jacket aside to reveal the butt of a gun. "We'll have fun with all of ya."

Then the guy turned in his chair and began to beckon to

the pair accompanying him. Except, the guy's henchmen were no longer standing a few feet behind him, leaning against the bar. Instead, Julian stood there, one arm on the bar and holding a glass of wine in the other hand.

Julian smirked at the human, saying, "They were called away unexpectedly."

"What the hell?" the guy snarled. "You two don't know who you're messin' with."

Considering they both sported French accents, Jean-Paul realized it didn't take a stretch for the asshole to realize they were together.

"The same can be said of you," Jean-Paul stated, a cold smile curving his lips as he met the angry human's gaze. "Run along, and don't bother Saul again."

Instead of responding to Jean-Paul, he turned his attention to Saul. "You know we don't take no for an answer, Saul," he stated on a growl. "You won't always have these Frenchies around to protect you."

Then the guy rose to his feet and began stalking away.

As Jean-Paul watched, Julian followed the man from the wine bar. He knew his enforcer would do what needed to be done to alter his memory about why he'd left. His man was excellent at not leaving loose ends.

"Who are you?" Saul asked once the pair had left the wine bar. "And why did you help me?"

Jean-Paul smiled at Saul, taking in the confusion in his expression and scent. After placing his wine glass on the table, he reached for the large human's hand. To Jean-Paul's pleasure, Saul allowed him to take his hand.

"I noticed you when you walked in," Jean-Paul admitted, smiling at him. "I was coming up with a suave opening line when I saw that man approach you." Barely refraining from curling his lip, since that would reveal a fang, Jean-Paul stated, "And it was easy to see you were not pleased to see him."

Saul rubbed the back of his neck with his free hand, then seemed to catch himself and moved it to twirl his wine glass instead. It was clear that he was trying to decide how to respond. He glanced at Jean-Paul, then at the wine, before returning his attention back to Jean-Paul.

"As grateful as I am for the intervention," Saul began slowly as he shifted his weight in his chair. "Getting involved, stopping Reagan like that, well" — Saul grimaced and sighed, returning his attention to the wine — "it's probably put you in danger. From your accent, I'm guessing you're French. A tourist?" He returned his attention to him and murmured, "If you're here long, Reagan might try to ambush you with plenty of back-up. Be careful until you leave."

Upon hearing Saul's obvious concern for his welfare, Jean-Paul couldn't resist confirming if Saul was indeed his beloved. "You are kind to be worried about me," he crooned as he squeezed Saul's hand lightly. He cradled the big male's between both of his own for a few seconds, massaging it. "But I can assure you, I am well able to take care of myself."

Jean-Paul held Saul's gaze as he lifted the man's hand to his lips. Gently, he placed a kiss to his palm. Then he opened his mouth a smidge and scraped a fang over the flesh below his thumb, pricking the skin just hard enough to draw a bead of blood. As Jean-Paul lapped at the tiny drop, he heard Saul inhale sharply, but he didn't pull away.

Saul's exquisite flavor burst across Jean-Paul's taste buds, and he barely resisted the urge to moan. Closing his eyes for just a second, he reveled in the knowledge that finally, after nearly three centuries, he had found the one — his beloved. Sitting in a wine bar, being harassed by an asshole, Jean-Paul found his beloved waiting for his aid.

Glad I ended up in Vegas instead of Savannah.

Finally feeling Saul tug at his hand, Jean-Paul opened his eyes and refocused on the human that was the other half of his soul.

"Did you just bite me?" Saul asked, furrowing his brows. He glanced at his friend. "That's what it felt like."

"Just enjoying your flavor," Jean-Paul replied honestly. After squeezing Saul's hand once more, he released the man. Resting one hand on the table near where Saul placed his hand, Jean-Paul picked up his wine with the other. "So, you called that asshole Reagan. What did he want?"

"Who are you?" Saul's friend asked, leaning his forearms on the table and scowling at him. "What's it to you?"

"Ah, my apologies." Jean-Paul chuckled softly as he realized that in the face of finding his beloved, he'd completely forgotten the niceties. "I am Jean-Paul Tremblay." He reached a hand across the table, holding Saul's friend's gaze. "And you are?"

"Marty," the human replied, taking Jean-Paul's hand. As they shook, he added, "Uh, Martin Jamison."

"Nice to meet you, Martin," Jean-Paul replied, releasing the human. Then he held out his hand to Saul. "Saul what?"

Saul glanced at Jean-Paul's hand, then back at his face, before meeting his gaze and once again taking his hand. "Saul Mandisa."

Jean-Paul peered into Saul's clear blue eyes as he lightly squeezed his beloved's hand. "Very nice to meet you, Saul Mandisa." Then he winked as he released his human's hand. "So very nice." Out of the corner of his eye, Jean-Paul noticed Julian joining them in the fourth chair. "This is my friend, Julian Allard."

"Gentlemen," Julian rumbled, but he didn't bother offering a hand to shake. Instead, he relaxed back in his seat and told him, "Caspian and Casey arrived. I told them we'd meet up with them tomorrow for brunch."

"Thank you, Julian," Jean-Paul replied, deciding brunch would come all-too-soon if it pulled him away from alone time with his beloved.

Of course, I need to convince him to join me for the evening first.

Hmmm . . . when was the last time I had to use words to coerce a human into my bed?

In truth, Jean-Paul couldn't remember.

For my beloved, I will succeed in this challenge.

"Did you just blow off your friends to sit with us?" Saul cocked his head, once more seeming confused. Then he smirked as he leaned toward him, sweeping his gaze up and down Jean-Paul's body before meeting his gaze again. "Are you trying to get laid, Jean-Paul?"

Hmmm . . . maybe it won't be so difficult.

"I am definitely interested in exploring every inch of your gorgeous frame, Saul," Jean-Paul confirmed, giving his beloved a heated look. "For hours."

Grinning, Saul rumbled, "Well, you did do me a solid, sending Reagan on his way." His blue eyes glimmered with heat as the scent of attraction rolled off his body. "I think sharing some time with you is the least I could do."

Jean-Paul figured it wasn't the most romantic of ways to pick up his beloved, but he would take it . . . and happily.

"Then why don't we enjoy our wine, share a little about ourselves, and then head to my hotel room?"

To Jean-Paul's amusement, Saul picked up his wine and downed the dark fluid in several gulps.

CHAPTER THREE

*O*kay, so that probably wasn't the classiest of moves, but god, my *dick is hard.*

The way Jean-Paul and his friend had sent Reagan and his buddies packing had been damn hot. Saul had never seen anyone handle Reagan in such a manner. Most people were intimidated by the guy, but Jean-Paul had seemed to be completely unimpressed with him.

Saul found it oddly hot.

"I take it that wine was really good," Jean-Paul commented, amusement in his tone.

Fighting back a flush of embarrassment, Saul cleared his throat. "Uh, sorry." He rubbed the back of his neck as he muttered, "Probably not the kind of class you're used to."

Jean-Paul's brown eyes appeared to twinkle as he replied, "No, and I find that quite refreshing."

With a wink, Jean-Paul picked up his stemware and lifted it to his lips. He held Saul's gaze as he followed Saul's lead and downed the rest of his glass in two gulps. Although, to be fair, Jean-Paul's glass didn't have a whole lot left in it, telling Saul the man had been there for a while.

"I'm not doing that," Julian grumbled as Jean-Paul placed the glass back on the table. Instead, he rose from his seat, taking his glass with him. Julian peered at Marty and smirked. "What about you, Marty? You're a good-looking guy. You interested in going a round with me?"

Saul grinned as Marty's cheeks turned a slight shade of pink. "Uh, I don't think I've had enough wine to swing your way."

Julian's gaze turned intense as he leaned toward Saul's friend. "You sure, Marty? I can guarantee you'd have a really, *really* pleasurable evening."

With wide eyes, Marty glanced at Saul, then Jean-Paul.

Jean-Paul shrugged. "I've heard that Julian's exceptional at bed-play."

Saul narrowed his eyes, as a hint of jealousy coiled within his gut, surprising him with its intensity. He couldn't recall ever feeling such a thing for a fling. The fact that Saul had just met the guy made his reaction that much odder.

As if Jean-Paul could read his mind, he swung his attention back to Saul and told him, "That's not something I have first-hand experience with." As Jean-Paul spoke, he reached out and took Saul's hand once more.

Saul couldn't remember any past pick-ups who'd been so touchy-feely. Still, he couldn't say he minded. It felt surprisingly nice.

"Uh . . ."

Upon hearing Marty's indecision, Saul turned his attention back to his friend. He could only recall the man hooking up with a guy once, and that had been a twink who'd offered to suck his cock. Marty had disappeared into the back for a few minutes and had returned looking more relaxed.

"Have a good time or not, man." Saul grinned at Marty. "You know you'll get no judgment from me."

To Saul's surprise, Marty licked his lips before clicking his tongue. Then he eyed Julian and asked bluntly, "You gonna suck my cock, Julian?"

Julian chuckled low in his throat, the sound holding a wealth of huskiness as he eased a step closer to Marty. "With pleasure," he rumbled, his dark eyes narrowing as he swept his gaze over Marty's body. "And I'll happily suck on other parts of you, too."

Saul startled a bit when he felt Jean-Paul slide his arm around his waist.

"Come on, Saul," Jean-Paul crooned into his ear. "Let's get moving. I'd very much like to get you alone so we can explore each other."

While Saul had never been held by a guy in his life, he didn't fight Jean-Paul's urgings as he slid his hand to his lower back. As he was guided out of the wine bar, Saul realized that while the man stood a couple of inches shorter than Saul's own six-foot-five, his personality made him seem larger. Jean-Paul moved with confidence as he turned to the left, heading down the strip.

People even moved out of his way.

Saul had never seen anything like it.

"How long have you lived in Las Vegas?" Jean-Paul asked conversationally. "Or have you always lived here?"

Saul felt a bit of surprise that Jean-Paul was making small talk. Most tricks didn't. He couldn't recall the last time he'd told personal information to a guy he'd fucked around with.

Still, Saul felt compelled to answer.

"Uh, I was born in Iowa," Saul admitted, glancing at Jean-Paul, seeing that the guy was watching him intently even as he continued to cause people to move out of his path. "I moved out here when I was twenty-one to work in show biz." With a shrug and a snort, Saul continued, "Turns out, I have two left feet, so that didn't work out."

"What do you do then?" Jean-Paul asked, still sounding damn curious.

"I work at *Emeril's* as a host and waiter," Saul revealed.

Cocking his head just a smidge, Jean-Paul wondered, "Do you enjoy your work?"

"Uh . . . sure." Saul couldn't fathom why Jean-Paul would question him about that. In need of a subject change, before Jean-Paul could ask something else, Saul posed one of his own. "What about you? Where in France are you from?"

"I live a bit north of Montpellier," Jean-Paul told him with a smile. "Know where that is?"

Saul chuckled as he shook his head. "Uh, no. Sorry."

"A gorgeous river basin with easy access to mountains in southern France." From the tone of his voice, Jean-Paul sounded fond — or maybe proud — of where he lived. "Do you enjoy hiking or biking? It's extremely popular in the area."

"I do enjoy hiking," Saul admitted slowly.

Is Jean-Paul insinuating that if I could ever get to France . . . that we could hook-up there?

Saul didn't know why Jean-Paul would make that kind of assumption. After all, they'd known each other all of ten minutes.

"I look forward to showing you a few trails," Jean-Paul stated, as if confirming Saul's confused thoughts. "I bet you'll love them."

After opening his mouth for a few seconds, Saul snapped it shut again.

Huh?

"This way," Jean-Paul urged, indicating that they begin moving toward the *Bellagio.*

"Of course, you have a room here."

"You don't care for the *Bellagio*?" Jean-Paul sounded curious. "I had read wonderful reviews about it."

Shit! Did I say that out loud?

Grimacing, Saul cast Jean-Paul a glance, taking in his arched brow, before returning his attention to the structure's impressive façade. "Uh, I've heard great things about it, too." Using his thumb to point over his shoulder, Saul added, "Love the dancing fountains. Have spent many an evening enjoying their choreography."

Jean-Paul peered in the direction of the fountains that graced what was essentially the front yard of the hotel, which faced the strip. "Then I look forward to watching it with you,"

Jean-Paul stated before turning what could only be called a feral smile upon Saul. "But tomorrow. I can't see us leaving my suite tonight . . . for any reason."

A shiver of arousal, anticipation, and even a smidge of uncertainty trickled down Saul's spine. Even though he was taller, broader, and had plenty more muscles than Jean-Paul, he suddenly felt as if he were prey. He couldn't ever remember feeling that way before, and he wasn't sure how he felt about it.

"Relax, my beloved Saul," Jean-Paul crooned, rubbing his hand up and down his spine soothingly. "Nothing will happen that you don't wish. Just as Julian would never do anything your friend, Marty, doesn't want."

Jean-Paul glanced over his shoulder, and Saul followed the action. He spotted Julian and Marty following them. They appeared to be engaged in conversation, Marty indicating the fountains.

Saul noticed that, unlike himself and Jean-Paul, the pair didn't touch, nor did they appear to be more than a couple of buddies catching up.

"Don't worry about your friend," Jean-Paul encouraged, teasing his fingertips over his lower back. "Julian will take wonderful care of him."

Saul nodded, even though he felt a little bad that concern for his buddy hadn't even crossed his mind.

"So, does your comment about the *Bellagio* mean you're impressed with it, then?"

Returning his attention to his hook-up for the evening, Saul admitted, "I've never seen any of the rooms in the *Bellagio*."

"Ahhhh." Jean-Paul smiled widely, pleasure lighting his dark eyes. "Then I look forward to spoiling you."

Amusement filling him, chasing away the unease, Saul teased, "What? Ya gonna order chocolate-covered strawberries, champagne, and whipped cream?"

Jean-Paul's eyes narrowed. "Hmmm . . . licking whipped cream off your dick." He lowered his attention to Saul's groin before meeting his gaze again. "What an excellent idea."

Saul opened his mouth, then closed it again, once more uncertain what to say.

When they entered the hotel, Saul glanced around curiously. The place screamed of opulence from the marble floor to the gilded ceilings. He peered right and noticed the opening to the gaming room, but Jean-Paul led the way to the left and a bank of elevators.

Evidently, the man noticed his interest, however, for he asked, "Do you have a favorite game?"

Barking a laugh, Saul shook his head. "Naw."

As Jean-Paul hit the *up* button for the elevator, he arched one brow in silent question.

Feeling his cheeks heat, Saul mumbled, "Can't afford to gamble away money."

Jean-Paul nodded once, his attention shifting to the opening elevator door. "It takes a truly self-aware man to be at one with one's surroundings." He slid his fingers between Saul's, pulling him into the elevator car. At the same time, he pointed toward the archway leading to the gaming room. "Especially in a place such as this."

Saul didn't know about that. He figured it had more to do with the fact that he didn't want to be broke all the time. Instead of voicing that thought, he kept it to himself.

"Let's go to the suite and get comfortable," Jean-Paul urged.

When Jean-Paul says suite, he truly means suite.

Barely resisting his urge to whistle, Saul paused mid-way into the front room and stared as he swept his gaze over the gorgeously appointed room. The space before him could have encompassed his tiny old apartment three times over. The carpet was rich, the furnishings lavish, and the curtains at the far end of the room had been left open, revealing a balcony as well as a fabulous view of the strip.

Marty didn't seem nearly as reticent. Saul heard him whistle loudly behind him, drawing his attention. He noticed how his buddy had his hands shoved into his pockets, and he stared around in wonder.

Turning to Julian, Marty asked, "What the hell do you guys do that you can afford this?"

Even as Saul's cheeks began to heat in embarrassment upon hearing Marty's bluntly asked question, Julian chuckled as he answered. "Well, we're very successful businessmen that hold the patents for quite a few inventions." As he spoke, Julian turned his attention to Jean-Paul. "Would that be an accurate description?"

"*Oui*," Jean-Paul replied with a nod, and even Saul knew that the word meant yes. Meeting Saul's gaze, he stated, "We are excellent at business."

Without another word, Jean-Paul took Saul's hand and began leading him toward a closed door on his left.

Anticipation flooded him when the lean, toned man opened the door, revealing a lavish bedroom suite. Except, it wasn't the gorgeously appointed room that drew Saul's attention. Instead, it was the huge California-king bed that barely filled the space.

Saul's nerves eased as arousal thrummed through him anew.

Hell, yeah.

CHAPTER FOUR

The scent of Saul's arousal flooded Jean-Paul's senses, causing his cock to throb within the confines of his slacks. Never in his life could he remember feeling so aroused. Even his fangs ached in a way he'd never before experienced as his mouth watered for a deeper taste of his beloved's tantalizing life-fluid.

Soon. So very soon.

Still, Jean-Paul wanted to fulfill his beloved's desire for treats. His need to spoil his big human was unexpected, but he didn't bother trying to ignore it. Besides, the idea of licking chocolate and whipped cream off of his soon-to-be lover's body filled Jean-Paul with even more anticipation.

Jean-Paul stared at Saul, watching his beloved take in the luxury of the suite. While his human attempted to appear unaffected, Jean-Paul knew better. He noticed his slightly increased heart rate, as well as the tiniest way Saul's lips parted, and his eyes widened before he caught himself.

Suppressing a smug smile, Jean-Paul picked up the phone's handset off the nightstand. After a glance down and hitting the button to connect with the concierge, he returned his perusal to Saul. There was just something so satisfying in knowing that he was standing in the room with his beloved.

"*Bellagio* concierge," a woman's voice greeted him. "How can I help you this evening?"

"Please bring to my room a bottle of champagne, two flutes, a half-dozen chocolate-covered strawberries, a bowl of whipped cream, and a warmed jar of caramel," Jean-Paul stated succinctly. As he spoke, he watched Saul pivot to stare at him, his jaw sagging a little.

"Do you think they even have all that on hand?" Saul murmured in clear disbelief.

So used to having his orders followed, the idea of what Jean-Paul wanted being unavailable hadn't even occurred to him.

To Jean-Paul's pleasure, after a couple of seconds of waiting, the woman replied, "Of course, sir." After she'd confirmed his room, she added, "We can have that to you in about fifteen minutes."

Planning to have Saul naked and writhing with pleasure within five, Jean-Paul countered, "No. Please bring it to my room in thirty minutes." He paused for just an instant before ordering, "Leave it on a wheeled cart outside the door. I will collect it myself."

"Yes, sir," she replied, without missing a beat. "I'll have that delivered as instructed."

"Thank you." Jean-Paul hung up the phone and refocused on Saul.

To his surprise, Saul was smirking at him. "Thirty minutes, huh?" he teased, shoving his hands into his pockets, drawing Jean-Paul's attention to his beloved's blatant erection trapped behind his fly. "I think it might take a little longer than that."

"Oh, no. You misunderstand me," Jean-Paul replied, stalking slowly toward Saul as he slipped out of his suit jacket and draped it across the back of the chair before the dressing table. "That will be just enough time to take the edge off our mutual lust."

"The edge off?" Saul whispered before he slipped out his tongue and traced it over his full bottom lip.

"*Oui, bien-aimé,*" Jean-Paul rumbled, calling his human beloved in his native tongue. While he noticed the slight furrowing of Saul's brows, he didn't stop to explain. Instead, as he slipped several top buttons free of their holes, Jean-Paul found his gaze riveted to Saul's full lips, his desire to taste them surging to a nearly irresistible level. "As we recover, we'll enjoy a drink, a treat, and some talk, before I take my time exploring every inch of your body," Jean-Paul vowed as he began closing the distance between them.

Coming to a stop before Saul, Jean-Paul skipped the rest of the buttons and eased his shirt over his head. He tossed it to the floor before gripping the hem of his undershirt. After removing that, too, he reached for the fly of his slacks.

"Wait," Saul rumbled, reaching for him. "Let me."

Jean-Paul smiled with pleasure, appreciating that Saul felt confident enough to participate. Even smaller than his beloved, he knew his dominant personality had made him a little hesitant. As Jean-Paul's beloved, his human would be welcome to touch him anywhere, anytime, not that Saul would know that, yet.

So much to explain.

Then Saul slid his fingers between the opened flaps of Jean-Paul's fly, caressing his silk boxer-covered erection.

Jean-Paul groaned softly, expressing his enjoyment of Saul's touch. Seeing his beloved glance at his face, he saw the question in his deep blue eyes even as he repeated the move. Sucking in a harsh breath, Jean-Paul growled softly as he offered his human a hungry look.

"Like I told you," Jean-Paul murmured huskily, his accent thickening as his arousal surged. "We will definitely need to take zee edge off."

As Jean-Paul spoke, he toed off his shoes. The move jostled Saul's hands, and his beloved eased back a step. Taking advantage, Jean-Paul swiftly shucked his boxers and slacks, taking his socks off along with them, before he straightened again.

Saul sucked in a sharp breath, his eyes darkening to a stormy blue as a fresh wave of his arousal teased at Jean-

Paul's senses. He'd obviously been removing his shirt as Jean-Paul had been finishing stripping, and the green polo dangled in his right hand. He stood frozen, his gaze riveted on Jean-Paul's lean torso.

"Gods, but you do smell intoxicating," Jean-Paul murmured as he took the shirt from Saul's grip and dropped it to the floor. "I love zat you're not wearing cologne."

Nothing marred Saul's unique scent beyond the subtle hint of soap, telling him that he'd showered recently.

As Jean-Paul reached for the fly of Saul's jeans, he spotted a hint of pink darkening the skin of his human's neck. The slightly spicy scent of embarrassment tainted the air. Saul even cleared his throat and looked away.

"I have said somezing wrong," Jean-Paul guessed, but that didn't stop him from easing Saul's jeans midway down his thighs. For the moment, he left his boxer-briefs in place so he could get to the bottom of the sudden change. Jean-Paul cleared his throat and focused. "Sit on the bed behind you, Saul," he encouraged, giving his hip a squeeze. "As I undress you, please tell me what just popped into your head."

"Uh, well," Saul began slowly even as he obeyed Jean-Paul and settled on the side of the bed. "It's just —"

Whatever it was, as Saul paused, Jean-Paul saw that he still sported a thick hard-on behind his underwear, which pleased him.

Once Jean-Paul had worked off Saul's shoes, socks, and jeans, he settled on his knees and rested his palms on his beloved's thick thighs. Gently, he urged his soon-to-be lover to spread his legs, pleased when Saul did so with barely any effort. Jean-Paul held Saul's gaze, waiting, albeit, impatiently.

"Saul?" he prodded softly, sliding his palms up his beloved's legs, finding his human's lightly-haired limbs tantalizing.

That will feel fantastic rubbing against my own.

"I forgot to put on deodorant," Saul blurted, his lips twisting in a grimace. "I'm sorry I smell."

"Hmmm." Jean-Paul hummed as he smoothly rose to his feet. "You misunderstand."

Jean-Paul gripped the outside of Saul's upper thighs. Using his heightened vampire strength, he eased his beloved backward, pushing him fully onto the bed. He immediately followed him, allowing him to position a clearly surprised Saul—judging by his scent and expression—into the middle of the bed. Jean-Paul levered over him, one knee beside Saul's hip and the other between his beloved's spread thighs.

Resting his weight on his hands, Jean-Paul leered at Saul. "I love how you smell." Then, to emphasize his point, he dipped down, pressed his nose into Saul's armpit, and inhaled deeply. With a groan, he muttered, "Perfectly masculine."

"Oh, shit," Saul muttered, even as he lifted his arm higher, offering Jean-Paul more room. "That's so fucking kinky, but hot as hell."

Jean-Paul chuckled huskily as he settled his left hand on Saul's torso and began tracing along his ribcage. His human was deliciously toned, allowing him to make out each bone under his fingertips. He counted down them until he found Saul's abdominals, where he traced along the delineated muscles there.

He reveled in the knowledge that his beloved was big and strong.

Able to handle a vampire master's lust.

Once Jean-Paul began teasing his fingertips under the waistband of Saul's boxer-briefs, he lifted his head and peered at Saul. He smiled, appreciating the look of lust darkening his features, all traces of embarrassment gone. Inhaling deeply, Jean-Paul noticed how Saul's heightened arousal caused his blood to pound in his veins, and his mouth watered with need even as his cock throbbed.

"Time to move this along, Saul," Jean-Paul rumbled as he discreetly grew the talon on the index finger of his left hand. "It's time we take care of that edge I mentioned."

Ever-so-carefully, with a bend of Jean-Paul's finger, he sliced through the fabric of Saul's underwear. He withdrew his talon as he turned his hand and gripped the fabric. A quick twitch of his wrist allowed Jean-Paul to rend them the rest of the way, baring Saul's beautiful erection to his gaze while drawing a gasp of surprise from his beloved.

His human was big in all areas, and Jean-Paul anticipated all the fun he was going to have with his human's massive tool.

As Jean-Paul wrapped his fingers around his human's thick, maybe eleven-inch erection, he used his left knee to urge his forever love's legs wider.

Saul spread his legs quickly. At the same time, he reached up and gripped Jean-Paul's upper arms. He began to pull, drawing him closer.

"Do you kiss?" Saul asked, eyeing Jean-Paul's lips.

In the past, Jean-Paul had considered kissing a means to an end if he didn't want to trance his blood donor. With the way he'd eyed Saul's lips, however, he knew that wouldn't be the case with his beloved. Kissing this human would be something he intended to do often.

"Even if I hadn't," Jean-Paul replied as he settled between Saul's legs. With a quick grin, he finished, "With you, I'd always make an exception."

While Jean-Paul noticed Saul blink once — probably in surprise upon seeing his pointed fangs — he didn't give him a chance to dwell on it. Instead, he peered between them and released Saul's dick. Ignoring his beloved's groan, Jean-Paul gently gripped his foreskin between his thumb and forefinger. He tugged it carefully and eased it over the head of Saul's circumcised cock.

A second later, Jean-Paul released himself and lowered his hips. He heard Saul's harsh inhale of breath, and he focused his gaze on his lover, gauging his reaction. His human's blue eyes were huge in his face, and he seemed to be staring in shocked wonder.

Even Saul's abdominals fluttered, as if he were struggling to remember to breathe.

Jean-Paul eased to his left elbow, pressing their bodies together from thighs to pecs. Uncertain of Saul's sensitivity, he started a slow rolling of his hips, stimulating them both. The first rock nearly went straight to Jean-Paul's head, and his own swift inhale matched the quick rise of Saul's chest when he gasped again.

As Jean-Paul finished the move, rocking his hips back again, Saul let out a low, throaty moan. His eyelids slid to half-mast as the big body beneath him shuddered hard. Then, to Jean-Paul's surprise, Saul tightened his hand on one arm while thrusting his second into his hair.

Saul finished the move by cupping Jean-Paul's head and pulling him toward him.

Had it been any other person, Jean-Paul would have resisted. For his beloved, however, he would give him anything. A second later, Jean-Paul was more than happy with the result as he found himself with a mouthful of Saul's enthusiastic tongue.

Opening wide and tilting his head, Jean-Paul fitted their mouths together more fully. He welcomed Saul's tongue, teasing it with his own. Sucking and nipping at it lightly, he drew blood, and Jean-Paul couldn't seem to find it in himself to care that his vampiric nature was getting the better of him.

With his beloved in his arms, nothing mattered but the feel of the man beneath him, the instinct to bond, and his desire to drive his human to the heights of ecstasy.

Instinct taking over, Jean-Paul took control of the kiss and sped up his rocking.

CHAPTER FIVE

The thought that he should be grossed out upon tasting his blood flitted through Saul's mind but only for an instant. He'd never been squeamish about that sort of thing. Besides, Jean-Paul's long canines made sense.

He likes bloodplay.

Saul had heard of people like that, but this was the first time he'd ever met one. While he supposed it would have been nice if the man had asked first, he didn't care all that much. Especially considering the fiery tendrils of pleasure coursing through his veins, all caused by this man's talented hands and uncircumcised cock.

Gripping Jean-Paul tightly, Saul bent his knees and planted his feet. He rolled his hips, crunching into each of his one-night stand's ruts. His balls tingled at the increased pressure, and he fed Jean-Paul a groan.

Jean-Paul growled back and pressed harder against him.

Saul bucked his hips, and he couldn't stop the shiver that zipped down his spine. His balls tingled, and he moaned once more. His release bowled over his senses, sending him soaring.

As the sweet bliss of his orgasm rolled over Saul, he turned his head, breaking the kiss. He panted harshly, riding the waves of pleasure. Saul stared vacantly at the wall as shudders vibrated his body again and again. His twitching cock throbbed in a delicious way that he'd never before experienced as his seed burst from him, only to get trapped within Jean-Paul's foreskin and ooze over his sensitive head.

Vaguely, Saul felt Jean-Paul begin kissing along his jaw and down his neck.

Smiling, Saul tipped his head back a little, offering more room. He found himself surprised by the affection, but he certainly wouldn't object. The way Jean-Paul's warm breath ghosted over his skin caused the hairs on his neck to stand on end, keeping the heat of arousal simmering through his veins.

An instant later, Saul registered the prick of teeth. To his surprise, while he felt just a flash of pain, it instantly disappeared. He recognized a sucking sensation to his neck, and it seemed to be the epicenter for a fresh wash of tingles that spread down his chest and shot straight to his groin.

Saul barked Jean-Paul's name as he was blind-sided by a second orgasm. His body trembled, his fingers spasming beyond his control as he clutched his lover's arms. He would have feared that he was squeezing too tightly if he could have dredged up a single thought.

Instead, Saul floated in ecstasy.

Slowly, Saul came back to himself. He opened eyelids he couldn't remember closing. After a few blinks, he managed to focus on the room.

Saul realized he still clutched at Jean-Paul's arms. The man remained sprawled across him, his lean, firm body warm against him. Saul felt Jean-Paul's lips mouthing kisses over his neck, and it caused goose bumps to spread down his arm.

Humming, Saul slowly began turning his head. The move dislodged Jean-Paul's lips, and the smaller man lifted his head. Instead of meeting the other man's gaze, Saul found his focus snagged by the white skin around where he clutched at his arms.

"Shit. Sorry," Saul muttered as he eased his grip. His fingers actually felt stiff, attesting to how tightly and for how long he must have been holding him. Grimacing, Saul murmured, "I'm so sorry, man. Didn't mean to hurt you."

After a second of hesitation, Saul rubbed at the marks he'd left behind, hoping to soothe the guy. He really didn't want to get thrown out of Jean-Paul's bed because he couldn't control his strength. Saul couldn't remember the last time that had happened.

Guess docking really does it for me.

And maybe that bloodplay.

That shit was crazy hot . . . and weird.

Saul wasn't certain why, but he had the odd impression that if it had been anyone else, he wouldn't have been pleased about getting bitten. With Jean-Paul, however, not only had it been amazing, but it had boggled his mind. Saul had come from it, which was beyond crazy.

"You may clutch at me any time you wish, *bien-aimé*," Jean-Paul crooned, his dark eyes glittering in the light of the room. "I'll always love wearing your marks."

Uncertain how to respond, Saul remained quiet as he continued to rub Jean-Paul's arms. *The guy is just being polite, right?* After all, they were enjoying a one-night stand.

The rich foreigner just wants a roll in the sack with an American while on vacation.

Except, Saul recalled Jean-Paul's comment about wanting to take him hiking near Montpellier, wherever that was.

Why would he be serious, though? He's a rich and obviously powerful French guy. What the hell could he possible see in me?

"You're thinking about that far too hard, *bien-aimé*," Jean-Paul murmured. Resting his weight on his forearms, he put a little space between them. After pecking Saul's lips, Jean-Paul stated, "Stay relaxed and still. This may feel a little weird."

Before Saul could fathom what Jean-Paul meant, the man eased farther away from him. At the same time, he reached his right hand between them. When Jean-Paul gripped Saul's semi-hard prick, he gasped in surprise.

A second later, Saul grunted as Jean-Paul rocked backward, the move separating their pricks.

"Damn," Saul hissed before blowing out a sharp breath. He eyed Jean-Paul's groin, glancing between it, his own, and back again. They were both speckled with drying white pools, although Jean-Paul's were dripping down his side as he rested next to him.

"Was that your first experience docking?" Jean-Paul asked softly, rubbing over Saul's penis gently.

Saul shifted his ass a little on the comforter, finding the fabric satiny soft. "Yeah," he admitted, trying to ignore the warm caress that was a mixture of stimulating and uncomfortable. With his brain-to-mouth filter misfiring, Saul blurted, "Uh, it's different."

Jean-Paul chuckled softly, proving he wasn't upset. Instead, he leaned over and pecked a kiss to Saul's lips. He put a little space between them and pinned him with an intense expression.

"It seemed as if you enjoyed it, though."

Nodding quickly, Saul confirmed. "Yeah."

"Good." Jean-Paul pecked his lips again before drawing way. "You get us a warm cloth, and I'll get the champagne."

"Okay."

After sliding from the bed, Jean-Paul grabbed the ruined boxer-briefs that he'd somehow managed to pull off of Saul. Saul still had no idea how the man had managed it. Especially since, as Saul watched Jean-Paul take a swift wipe across his groin, he noticed the briefs hadn't been torn along a seam.

Jean-Paul winked at him before dropping the ruined clothes in favor of grabbing his discarded slacks. When the man turned and bent, showcasing his ass beautifully while pulling them on, Saul nearly swallowed his tongue. He must have made some noise, for Jean-Paul turned while zipping and buttoning and pinned him with a narrow-eyed gaze.

"Hmmm. You want my ass." Jean-Paul actually sounded . . . surprised. He even tipped his head to the side a little as if analyzing him for a moment. Finally, he murmured, "That could be interesting."

Latching onto that, Saul eased to a sitting position and swung his legs over the side of the bed. "You not a bottom, Jean-Paul?"

"Let's just say . . . it's been a lot of years," Jean-Paul told him with a small smile. With a wink, he turned and headed toward the door, stating over his shoulder, "I'll be right back, *bien-aimé*."

As Saul rose to his feet and padded into the bathroom, he made a mental note to ask what that meant. When learning a second language had been a requirement in high school, he'd chosen Spanish. He'd had a Spanish girlfriend, at the time, and had wondered what the hell she'd been saying to her friends on the phone.

As it had turned out, Saul was about as good at learning languages as he was with dancing. He'd learned just enough to pass his tests with a C-average. The few phrases Saul had learned hadn't given him much insight into the girl's conversations, and they'd broken up while in his second quarter.

Too bad I didn't choose French.

With a roll of his eyes—*as if that would make any difference to this rich guy*—Saul flipped on the light switch. He froze, whistling low under his breath. Unable to help himself, Saul had to take a few minutes to admire the massive jetted tub, the huge shower with rainfall heads, and the thick fluffy bathrobes hanging across from the dual vanity.

"So this is how the other half lives," Saul whispered, knowing he would never be able to afford even one night in a room like this. "Not unless I win the lottery."

"You have won the lottery."

Spinning, Saul gaped at Jean-Paul. The man had already removed his slacks, and he leaned against the nearby dresser. A rolling trolley laden with items waited beside him.

"Uh, what?" Saul knew it was sort of an inane response,

but he found his focus stalled by the beautiful specimen of maleness before him. Plus, the guy was hard again already.

And he has such a pretty prick.

"The lottery. You won." Jean-Paul closed the distance between them, slipping past him. "At least, I think you'll believe that once I explain all the facts to you."

"The facts?" Saul would have felt embarrassed that he kept repeating the other man, but his dick was hardening again, and Jean-Paul was just so damn pretty. Sucking in a sharp breath, Saul shook his head once. "Um, you're going to have to explain that."

"Of course, Saul." Jean-Paul grabbed a dry, folded washcloth from a shelf as he turned on the water. "Do you know how to open a bottle of champagne?"

"Yeah." Saul felt relief that, as a waiter, it was something he had extensive experience with. Turning toward the cart and the bottle and flutes resting upon it, he headed that way. "I'll take care of it."

Saul turned away from the provocative sight to focus on the task assigned him. As he picked up the bottle, he read the label. Feeling impressed once again, knowing it was a damn fine vintage, Saul carefully popped the cork. Tilting a flute, Saul poured carefully, doing his best to control the carbonation.

He'd just placed the second glass on the tray when he felt a hand on his hip, nearly making him jump and knock over the flute.

"Sorry, *bien-aimé*," Jean-Paul murmured, rubbing soothingly over Saul's hip. "Didn't mean to startle."

Saul flashed a smile at the other man. "Been meaning to ask what that means. Uh, *bien-aimé*."

Jean-Paul smiled, his expression appearing surprisingly . . . fond.

"Uh, I just mangled that, didn't I?" Saul rubbed the back of his neck under his hair.

"A little bit," Jean-Paul conceded with a wink. "Don't worry. I'll teach you my language."

Again, Saul got the distinct impression that he was missing something.

Taking the flute Jean-Paul offered him, Saul decided he really needed to think with his big head. "Thank you," he murmured as he also snagged the damp towel the man was holding out.

Saul held Jean-Paul's gaze as he rubbed the towel over his stomach, abdominals, and groin, clearing away the evidence of their earlier releases. A glance down told him that Jean-Paul appeared clean, but he offered it to the man anyway. When Jean-Paul took it and gave himself a cursory swipe, Saul looked away and finally took a sip of the champagne.

Huh. Not bad, although the carbonation is a little rough.

Saul didn't drink sodas, and he wasn't used to the bubbles.

Dismissing that, Saul returned his attention to Jean-Paul and found the man staring at him with an intense and almost expectant look.

"You want to tell me something, don't you," Saul guessed softly, understanding that expression. "You want something."

"You are an extremely astute human, *bien-aimé*," Jean-Paul replied with a nod. "I feel so very blessed to call you mine."

Saul swallowed hard, confused by those words. "Human?" he whispered. Recalling the bloodplay, he guessed, "Do you think you're a vampire?"

"Not *think*," Jean-Paul countered as he narrowed his eyes. "How do you know about vampires?"

Saul chuckled softly as he touched his own teeth. "Come on. You altered your teeth, you bit my tongue, and you drank from my neck." Saying that out loud, Saul felt a fissure of unease slither up his spine. "You're into the whole *vampire culture*." He made air quotes with his free hand.

Jean-Paul's brows shot up for a second, then lowered again

just as quickly. "Ah, you think I'm role-playing." He nodded once. "Okay. Please, let me take this for just a second."

To Saul's surprise, Jean-Paul took his champagne flute and set it aside. Then he held up his hand. "Could a fake vampire do this?"

Before Saul's eyes, the nails on Jean-Paul's hand . . . changed. They lengthened into three-inch talons that appeared razor sharp. Gasping, Saul snapped his attention to Jean-Paul's face, ready to question him, only to find himself looking into a pair of red-irised eyes.

"Oh, fuck me," Saul whispered.

"I intend to," Jean-Paul stated calmly.

Saul gaped, uncertain how to respond . . . until his eyes rolled into the back of his head, and he dropped.

CHAPTER SIX

In hindsight, Jean-Paul realized he probably should have waited until Saul was sitting down to spring those changes on him. The way his big beloved gaped like a fish was completely expected. How his beautiful blue eyes rolled to the back of his head before he dropped like a stone was not.

Jean-Paul caught Saul with an arm around his waist. Stepping into the man caused his beloved to flop against his torso. Clutching his human close, Jean-Paul set his flute on the cart before easing that arm under Saul's legs and hefting him against his chest.

As Jean-Paul carried Saul to the bed, he realized that if he hadn't been a vampire, there was no way he would have been able to lift his beloved. He laid his human on the comforter, then moved him around so he could pull the blankets over him. His gorgeous human was a large male, weighing in around two-hundred-fifty pounds, and it was all muscle.

Taking a moment to trace over Saul's thick bicep, Jean-Paul admired his unconscious beloved. Fate had certainly been kind to him. He hoped the easy-going attitude his human had displayed at the wine bar, then in bed, would hold true to other areas of his life.

Jean-Paul had been alive a long time, and he knew he was a little set in his ways. As he noticed Saul's eyes begin to flutter behind his lids and a slight hitch in his breathing, he realized his beloved was waking. Soon, it would be time to explain vampires, and Jean-Paul wanted his beloved to be comfortable for that.

With that thought in mind, Jean-Paul swiftly wheeled the cart close to the side of the bed. He eased onto the mattress, slipping beneath the covers. Sitting beside his human, he adjusted the pillows behind him so he could rest his back against the headboard.

Then Jean-Paul picked up his champagne and took a sip, waiting and watching.

It didn't take long.

Saul's eyelids eased open, closed, then opened once more. His brows furrowed, and he looked a little confused as he glanced around. When Saul's gaze landed on Jean-Paul, his eyes widened right before he bolted into a sitting position.

"Easy, Saul," Jean-Paul crooned, rubbing up and down his beloved's back, disappointed to find so much tension there. "You're okay," he assured, hoping to soothe the man. "I would never hurt you."

Grimacing, Saul muttered, "I can't believe I fainted." He heaved a sigh as he rubbed his palms over his face. With a shake of his head, Saul grumbled, "May as well take away my fucking man card."

While surprised *that* was what Saul seemed upset about, Jean-Paul was pleased, too. He hoped Saul's concern didn't change when he reminded him of why he'd fainted. Jean-Paul knew it couldn't wait, either, needing his beloved to understand the important changes that were taking place in his life.

"Considering you just learned that vampires exist, and you're being bedded by one, it's no surprise that your mind needed a moment to catch up."

Saul swallowed so hard that his Adam's apple bobbed. "Vampire." He swept his gaze over Jean-Paul's face and torso. "Right." Pointing beyond him, Saul asked, "Think I can have that drink now? Although, something stronger wouldn't go amiss."

"I could order something," Jean-Paul offered as he handed

Saul the drink. With a wry smile, he added, "But I'd rather have you sober once explanations are done, because I want you to remember every second of me claiming you."

After taking a large gulp of the champagne, nearly draining the flute, Saul focused on Jean-Paul. He turned and began adjusting his pillows so Jean-Paul quickly gave him a hand. A few seconds later, Saul leaned against the pillows, turning a little to focus on him.

"Okay." Saul scrubbed a hand through his hair, pushing the thick blond strands away from his face and tucking it behind his ear. "I figure you decided to tell me that you're a vampire for a reason." Then Saul's eyes widened. "Oh, shit. You bit me. Does that mean I'm going to turn into one?"

Jean-Paul chuckled as he quickly shook his head. "No, *bien-aimé*. A vampire must be born. A human cannot be turned into one," he assured. Reaching over, he took Saul's free hand. "I'm telling you about vampires because, in my culture, you are someone very special . . . to me."

"I am?" Saul's skepticism rang through in his tone. "Special, how?"

"Well." Jean-Paul paused, gathering his thoughts, needing to present the information in the best light. "You see, vampires live a very long time. Upward of five hundred years."

"Damn," Saul mumbled. "That's a while."

Jean-Paul nodded. "It is, and it can get very lonely." He squeezed Saul's hand before explaining, "To alleviate that, Fate grants each paranormal a *bien-aimé*."

"That's what you've been calling me," Saul cut in, cocking his head. "What is it?"

"A beloved," Jean-Paul explained. Knowing his human would need more—and there was so much more to explain— he quickly added, "A beloved is the term a vampire uses to describe their—" Hesitating, Jean-Paul searched his mind for the proper words. "Soul mate . . . the one person we can bond with. Share our life with. The one who will complete us."

Saul's eyes narrowed as he mulled that over, taking a sip of champagne, probably to buy himself time. "You, uh, you sort of make it sound like, well, a spouse?"

"*Oui*." Jean-Paul quickly nodded. "Similar but with a few differences."

"And you've been calling me your *bien-aimé*," Saul mused, his brows furrowing. Meeting Jean-Paul's gaze, he asked, "You think I'm your, uh, this beloved soul mate thing?"

Unable and unwilling to ever deny his beloved, Jean-Paul nodded. "I don't just *think* you are my soul mate, Saul." He needed his human to understand that there was no guessing in this. "When I caught your scent at the wine bar, I was drawn to you like I never have been to another," he admitted. Turning Saul's hand and bringing it to his mouth, Jean-Paul kissed the flesh of his palm where he'd first nicked him at the restaurant. "I could not resist the allure of tasting your blood, even while out in public." Smiling, he added, "I'm so very impressed by how relaxed you were about it, and from your taste, I knew you were mine. Getting you here, alone, to share everything with you, to start our bond, to get to know you . . . it was all I could think about."

Realizing he was doing something he hadn't done in . . . centuries, rambling, Jean-Paul snapped his mouth shut and waited eagerly for Saul's response.

Saul inhaled deeply, then let it out through pursed lips, which he licked a second later, drawing Jean-Paul's attention. He recalled how delectable his beloved had tasted, how his human hadn't minded when he'd touched his fang to his tongue and enjoyed a little blood in their kiss. Jean-Paul had never done that with another, and his mouth watered with his desire to share that experience with him again.

"You're looking at me like you want to eat me," Saul mumbled, a hint of trepidation entering his scent. "And with you being a vampire, that sorta takes on a whole new meaning."

"You are completely safe with me, Saul," Jean-Paul assured once more, squeezing his hand. "You are now the most important person in my life." Needing to impress his seriousness, Jean-Paul added, "I would destroy anyone who attempts to come between us."

"Why?" Saul asked bluntly. "Why me?"

Jean-Paul paused, giving that the thought it deserved. "There are theories about how Fate chooses our beloveds," he began slowly. "But no one knows for certain." Seeing the confused disbelief in Saul's eyes, Jean-Paul quickly continued. "But I do not care about the *why*, Saul. All I care about is that after nearly three centuries of searching, I have finally found you. You are now my life."

Saul's blond brows furrowed as he continued to stare at him. Jean-Paul could practically see the wild thoughts spinning through his human's mind. He knew the acceptance of paranormals could be difficult for some humans, and he appreciated that his human wasn't yet running for the door.

Once again, Jean-Paul appreciated Saul's seemingly easygoing nature.

Fate is damn smart.

"So, if I'm your beloved, and you'll do anything for me," Saul began slowly, rubbing his thumb along the thin glass of the stemware. "You'll uproot your life in France and move here to be with me?"

Well, that is unexpected.

Jean-Paul hesitated an instant. "That wouldn't be my first choice," he admitted before draining the rest of his champagne. "More?" he asked as he placed his flute on the cart he'd positioned by the bed. "There is more to explain."

"Why am I not surprised," Saul muttered. Then he finished his drink and handed him the glass.

While Jean-Paul wasn't certain to what Saul was referring—there was more to explain or that moving to Vegas wasn't his first choice — he dutifully refilled their glasses. After returning the flute to Saul, he lifted the lid from a bowl to find whipped cream within it. Another contained the chocolate-covered strawberries, while a third held the caramel sauce.

Picking up a chocolate-covered strawberry, Jean-Paul swiped it through the whipped cream, scooping up a large dollop. He turned back to Saul. Resting his right hand on his beloved's thick upper bicep, Jean-Paul brought the treat to his human's lips.

"Bite?" Jean-Paul crooned, hoping to entice him.

Saul held his gaze for a heartbeat before opening his mouth.

Jean-Paul carefully eased half the dessert into Saul's mouth, holding the item steady as his beloved bit into it. As he lowered the sweet fruit, he watched his human chew. A bit of strawberry juice clung to the corner of Saul's lips.

Unwilling to deny himself, Jean-Paul leaned forward. He stuck out his tongue and licked it from his beloved, tasting his human and the dessert. Humming appreciatively, Jean-Paul winked at Saul before popping the remainder of the chocolate-covered strawberry into his own mouth.

After swallowing, Saul commented, "So, the myth that vampires only drink blood isn't true." Then he added, "Plus, I saw you drink wine and champagne. What else isn't true?" Saul glanced toward the window and the darkness illuminated by the lights of the strip. "Can you go out in sunlight?"

After swallowing his mouthful, Jean-Paul answered, "Pretty much the only myth that is true is the one where we require blood to survive." He reached for another strawberry, dipping it in caramel that time. Returning to Saul and bringing the food to his beloved's lips to bite, Jean-Paul continued, "I love garlic, holy water doesn't do a thing, enjoy sunbathing nude, and drive a stake through anyone's heart and they'll die."

Saul coughed once on his bite of food before mumbling around his mouthful, "You like to sunbathe nude?"

Jean-Paul chuckled softly as he gave Saul a heated smile. "*Oui*, Saul. I do." With a shrug, he added, "And the reason moving here wouldn't be my first choice is because I am the leader of my coven, Saul." Touching his chest, Jean-Paul added, "I am the Master Vampire of the Montpellier coven. Moving would be . . . difficult." He reached out and traced his fingertips along Saul's strong jawline. "You are the beloved of the master, Saul Mandisa. Every vampire within my coven will be overjoyed that I've finally found you, and they will be devoted to your happiness."

As Jean-Paul watched, Saul swallowed so hard his Adam's apple bobbed. "Wow."

CHAPTER SEVEN

Well, damn. I caught the eye, or scent, of not only a vampire, but a master vampire. How the hell is that even possible? Of all people, why me?

Unable to keep his thoughts completely to himself, Saul whispered, "I'm a nobody, Jean-Paul. You could do so much better than me."

"You are *not* a nobody," Jean-Paul countered, frowning at him. "You are the beloved of the master," he repeated. "You are the most important person in the world to me and to those in my coven." Then Jean-Paul's dark eyes narrowed as he added, "And if they don't agree, they can find a new coven."

"You'd kick them out if they didn't like me?" Saul gaped at Jean-Paul. "Why would you do that?"

"Because you are my beloved, Saul." Jean-Paul let out a soft sigh, and he furrowed his brows. Holding Saul's gaze, he shook his head. "Without you, I am nothing. I will cease to exist."

"Uh, wait." Saul couldn't have heard that right. "Did you just say you'll cease to exist? As in . . . die?"

Jean-Paul sighed deeply, his expression clouding over as he focused on the comforter.

Disquiet oozed through Saul upon seeing Jean-Paul express anything other than confidence.

"I shouldn't have said that," Jean-Paul murmured, but he wasn't taking back the words. Instead, he all but confirmed them by saying, "I'd hoped you would accept me without me having to share that first."

"Okay, you're going to have to explain," Saul insisted. It was his turn to reach out and take Jean-Paul's hand. "Share what? What did you mean?"

After letting out another deep sigh, Jean-Paul lifted his head and met Saul's gaze. "Now that I've met you, I can only feed from you, *bien-aimé*," he whispered softly. "Without you, I'll slowly starve to death."

"Well, shit," Saul mumbled, frowning. "Fate sure don't mess around, does she?" Shaking his head, he grumbled, "Bitch doesn't give you a choice."

Jean-Paul's lips curved into a small smile. "I wouldn't want a choice, Saul." He squeezed Saul's hand and told him, "Whatever our differences turn out to be, I'm certain that we will be able to work them out and that you will be perfect for me."

"No pressure," Saul quipped, rubbing the back of his neck.

Cocking his head, Jean-Paul told him, "Exactly. I didn't want to pressure you."

Realizing Jean-Paul hadn't understood, Saul didn't correct him. "Hand me another chocolate-covered strawberry with whipped cream," he requested instead. Saul smiled as he admitted, "I need a minute to process all this."

And if there's more, I'm not ready to hear it.

Jean-Paul immediately gave him the requested item. As Saul enjoyed the food, he watched the vampire refill his champagne flute. Saul wasn't entirely certain when he'd drained it, but he appreciated the gesture.

Instead of handing Saul the next strawberry, Jean-Paul once again hand-fed him. He vaguely wondered if the vampire master had ever done that with another. Deciding he didn't want to hear about it if Jean-Paul had, Saul kept the question to himself.

Appreciating that Jean-Paul remained quiet as he fed Saul, treating him as if he were something special, Saul allowed his thoughts to spin.

The man—vampire—before him was telling him that not only had Fate decided he was his perfect other half, but Jean-Paul didn't have a say in the matter. Saul had a funny feeling that he did have a choice, but not choosing Jean-Paul would be a death sentence for the man, and the vampire hadn't intended to share that.

Saul appreciated the slip of the tongue because if he'd ever found out that Jean-Paul had died without his blood, he never would have been able to live with himself.

Guess I've made my decision. I can't let this amazing man die just because I can't wrap my head around this insta-pairing thing.

"Jean-Paul," Saul started slowly, realizing there was one important thing he needed to know. "You talked about bonding." When Jean-Paul nodded, Saul continued, "What is that, and how is it done?"

Jean-Paul stared at him, his brows lifting a little to betray his surprise. Then a small smile curved his thin lips. "Guess I did miss that, didn't I?"

Rolling his shoulder in a half-shrug, Saul commented, "There seems to be a lot. I bet we've missed other stuff."

"Very true," Jean-Paul conceded, his smile widening. Then his gaze heated as his attention lowered to Saul's bare chest. "Bonding is done through sex. I will spill my seed in you and give you a claiming bite." Touching the skin where Saul's neck met his shoulder, Jean-Paul stated, "Here."

A slight tingle erupted from where Jean-Paul touched Saul, and the skin of his arms goose bumped. "D-Didn't you already bite me there?" Confused by the response, he pressed, "Does that mean you already started the process?"

Jean-Paul blew out a soft breath as he lowered his hand. Grimacing, he nodded once. "Technically, for me, the bonding process started the second I tasted your blood in the wine bar."

"But not for me?" Saul mused.

Shaking his head slowly, Jean-Paul admitted, "It's why I

wanted to take the edge off, then spend a few minutes talking to you." He rubbed along Saul's arm, tracing his musculature. "I wanted you to know what you were getting into."

The hairs on Saul's arm stood on end in reaction to Jean-Paul's touch. He cleared his throat, shifting his hips a bit on the bed. Saul hadn't quite softened to half-mast after his double-orgasm, which was just crazy, and he was swiftly boning up the rest of the way.

"Uh, okay. Guess I do now." Scoffing, Saul shook his head as he smiled wryly and admitted, "With Reagan sniffing around, I'd already been thinking about moving, even though I'd hoped I wouldn't have to." Seeing the concern enter Jean-Paul's dark eyes, Saul quickly barked a laugh and continued, "Although France was never on my radar. My friends are going to think I'm nuts for doing this."

"You can't tell them about us."

Upon hearing the concern in Jean-Paul's quickly spoken words, Saul nodded. "Oh, yeah. Of course." He had already figured that part out. "Oh, what about Marty?" Saul asked curiously, glancing toward the bedroom door. "Is he going to know since, uh, I guess I'm just assuming that Julian is a vampire like you?"

"Julian is a vampire," Jean-Paul confirmed. "He's my head enforcer. He's here watching my back while I'm on vacation." Chuckling softly, he added, "Julian wanted to bring another enforcer and a tracker, too, but I nixed that idea. The people I'm meeting here are all very capable and trustworthy vampires, and if I need more protection, they'd be perfectly capable of supplying it." Then Jean-Paul sobered as he added, "Although now that I've met my beloved, I wish I'd agreed with Julian."

"Why?" The word was out of Saul's mouth before he could think better of it. "Shit. Am I allowed to ask stuff like that?"

Perhaps the guy didn't like being questioned.

To Saul's relief, Jean-Paul smiled at him. "You may ask me anything you wish, *bien-aimé*." He set aside his glass and took Saul's empty one, placing it on the tray, too. "I like that you're interested."

Then Jean-Paul gripped Saul's hips and slid him down the bed a little. A second later, he pulled one of the pillows out from behind his back. Urging Saul down, Jean-Paul levered over him.

"Damn. You're a lot stronger than you look," Saul blurted, staring up at him in surprise. When Jean-Paul grinned, he added, "Guess that explains how you got me into bed when I fainted."

As Saul said the words, he felt his cheeks heat a little. He still couldn't believe he'd done that.

Jean-Paul rested his weight on his right forearm, easing the fingers of that hand into Saul's hair. "Julian would have told me if Marty was his beloved." As he continued speaking, he skimmed the backs of his fingertips along Saul's jaw, making it difficult to concentrate on his words. "Marty will only remember that he had a fantastic night, not that Julian drank his blood."

That caught his attention.

Wait. What?

"How's that possible?"

"Under most circumstances, a vampire has the ability to mentally manipulate a human's mind," Jean-Paul explained, scratching along Saul's scalp, causing the hairs on his nape to stand on end pleasantly. "Julian can use that to blur Marty's memories a bit. Your friend will recall having a fantastic night with Julian, but not that he's been fed upon."

When Jean-Paul lightly slid his fingertips over where he'd bitten Saul the first time, a pleasant shiver went down his spine to settle in his balls. Needing to do a little touching of his own, he reached up and wrapped his arms around Jean-Paul's lean torso. His new lover—*holy shit, I have a vampire for a lover* — smiled and eased their bodies against each other, reminding Saul that they were both nude.

Feeling the hot body nestled against him, Saul nearly missed Jean-Paul's next words.

"A vampire's saliva has natural healing properties," Jean-Paul told him. "Julian will lick over his bite mark, sealing it, and by morning, it will be gone."

"That makes sense," Saul muttered, smoothing his palms over Jean-Paul's back, feeling the strong lines there. "Otherwise, there would be a lot of unexplained bite reports out there."

"Exactly," Jean-Paul crooned as he lowered his head, clearly angling for a kiss. Before his lips touched Saul's, he paused and rocked his hips. "So, do you accept me, Saul?" Before Saul could answer, Jean-Paul stared at him with need and hunger in his expression. "May I make love to you and bond us for the rest of our days?"

"Yeah," Saul agreed, his attention falling to Jean-Paul's lips. "Yes, I agree to bonding." Just to be clear, he added, "To moving, to spending the rest of my days at your side." Then Saul pushed his head back into the pillow so he could focus fully on Jean-Paul's eyes as something popped into his head. "Wait a minute. You don't expect me to be the little woman, right? Sitting at home, cooking and cleaning, waiting for the man to come home at the end of the day?"

That so will not fly.

"No, absolutely not, *bien-aimé*." Jean-Paul's gaze remained steady upon him when he told him, "I work out of an office at the estate. If you want to learn the business with me, to run it at my side, I will teach you everything."

Saul couldn't hide his grimace fast enough upon hearing that offer. The idea of spending his days behind a desk sounded like torture. As lowbrow as many considered a waiter position, Saul liked it because it constantly kept him on the move.

Evidently, Jean-Paul caught on to Saul's complete lack of interest. He chuckled and grinned widely. "Of course, the coven lives on a massive estate with horses, cows, pigs, chickens, goats." He winked and told him, "I'm certain there will be some duty that will interest you."

"Really?" Saul wouldn't have guessed that. "Why all the animals?"

"We raise a lot of our own food," Jean-Paul revealed. Lowering his head, he whispered into Saul's ear. "There's also a greenhouse and a few small fields of wheat and corn."

When Jean-Paul suckled lightly on Saul's earlobe for a few seconds, a shiver rolled through him, and he clutched tighter at the lean vampire.

"Would you like to keep discussing the estate?" Jean-Paul asked in a throaty purr. Lowering a hand under the comforter, he wrapped his fingers around Saul's erection and gave it a slow stroke. "Or perhaps, you'd like to enjoy something a little less coherent."

Saul groaned and rocked his hips, pushing into each of Jean-Paul's firm strokes. "D-Definitely less c-coherent." Wanting to move things in that direction, Saul demanded, "Where's your lube?"

CHAPTER EIGHT

Jean-Paul's heart soared upon hearing Saul's words. His beloved had accepted him, accepted his nature, and wanted to bond with him. He felt blessed beyond all reason.

More than ready to facilitate Saul's request, Jean-Paul groaned as he eased away from his beloved. "Gotta get it."

Even as Jean-Paul moved away from Saul, he noticed an interesting scent erupt from Saul, and it took him a few seconds to place it.

Relief, but why?

As Jean-Paul headed into the bathroom, he glanced over his shoulder and commented, "Another interesting fact of vampires is that, along with increased strength, we have a heightened sense of smell." Able to see Saul as he fished through his half-unpacked bathroom bag, he added, "That gives many of us the ability to figure out what a person is feeling through their scent." While Jean-Paul watched his beloved's brows shoot up, he told him, "That means I can tell that you just thought of something that made you feel relief, and I'm wondering why." Just as Jean-Paul spoke the words, an unsettling idea entered his mind. "Does it mean you appreciate the reprieve caused by me having to get the lube and you need more time before we bond?"

Gods, that would suck, and not in the way I like.

Jean-Paul paused a few feet from the bed, lube in hand, as he waited for Saul's response. If he drew too close, he feared he wouldn't be able to give his beloved the time he needed if he did, indeed, ask to wait. His human's scent drew him like a moth to a flame, and he desperately wanted to bask in the heat of the man's body.

To Jean-Paul's surprise, Saul's scent took on a slightly embarrassed spice.

"You can tell what I'm thinking by scent?"

Saul didn't sound too pleased, so Jean-Paul simply nodded once.

"Damn," Saul muttered before blowing out a breath. Holding up a hand, his palm up in obvious invitation, he stated, "I wasn't relieved because I want to wait. My cock is so hard, and I wanna milk you so bad." Scoffing, Saul stated ruefully, "Never done it bare, and I'm lookin' forward to feelin' ya take me raw."

Taking Saul's hand, Jean-Paul allowed his human to lead him back onto the middle of the bed. He squelched his urge to growl upon hearing his beloved mention those in his past. Instead, Jean-Paul focused on the second part of his comment, how he looked forward to their impending coupling.

"Then why were you relieved?" Jean-Paul pressed. Seeing the way Saul looked away, he used his knees to push apart his beloved's thighs as he levered over him, resting his weight on the hand holding the lube. Jean-Paul cupped Saul's jaw with his free hand, urging his beloved to meet his gaze. "I know we're still learning about each other, so communication is extremely important."

Saul rolled his eyes before meeting Jean-Paul's gaze. "I was relieved that your lube wasn't in the nightstand or even in the bedroom." After a second of hesitation, he added, "Because that means you most likely haven't had anyone else in this bed, yet."

With a possessive growl, Jean-Paul grinned at Saul. "You're right about that. I haven't picked up anyone while here." Jean-Paul chose not to share that he'd only flown in that morning, and this was his first night there. Instead, he told him, "And you will be the only one I have in my bed ever again." Realizing he needed to clarify something else, Jean-Paul declared, "And if anyone tries to touch you, it will be the last thing they ever do."

To Jean-Paul's surprise, Saul grinned broadly. "Vampires are possessive, huh?"

Jean-Paul's tension eased from him just that fast. "Only for our beloved," he admitted. Realizing another fun fact he had to share, Jean-Paul admitted, "Like many covens, mine has a harem of donors that live with us. In exchange for a comfortable life and a wage, they provide the vampires of the coven with their blood."

"Harem?" Saul repeated, his eyes narrowing. "As in, they sleep with everyone . . . including you?"

Unwilling to lie to Saul, Jean-Paul nodded. "I have used their services when it's convenient, but the donor has the option of saying no to any vampire that doesn't interest them, and their choice has to be respected."

Sneering, Saul grumbled, "As if someone would ever deny the master of the coven."

Even as Jean-Paul mentally reveled in the jealousy emanating from his beloved, he told him, "Actually, there has been a time or two. If a donor doesn't want to sleep with men, his choice is respected." Still scenting Saul's irritation, Jean-Paul tried to think of what to say to get the evening back on track. He recalled how his beloved had responded when he'd sucked on his ear. Leaning close, he nuzzled his cheek against his human's while whispering, "That was all in the past, *bien-aimé*. Never again will I have anyone but you, and that knowledge thrills me."

Jean-Paul opened his mouth and suckled lightly, working his beloved's sensitive lobe. At the same time, he skimmed his free hand down Saul's chest, mapping his large pectoral. He teased his thumb over his human's nipple, enjoying the way it beaded beneath his ministration.

Saul groaned and shuddered beneath Jean-Paul. His arms tightened around his torso, cradling his shoulder blades. With a low moan, he seemed to melt into the mattress even as his arousal cocooned them, the finest of aphrodisiacs.

"Fucking hell," Saul whined, shuddering beneath him. He dug his nails into Jean-Paul's skin, holding him close. "Dumb response, I know, being jealous." Even though Saul panted the words, Jean-Paul was still able to make them out. "Neither of us are virgins, but it's just us from here on out, right?"

Jean-Paul relished the idea of wearing his beloved's marks, and he wondered if he could get his beloved to grow his nails a little longer. He released his human's lobe and began working his way down his beloved's neck, licking and sucking in equal measure.

"Correct," Jean-Paul crooned against his beloved's warm flesh. "Neither of us were virgins." Lifting his head a little, he met Saul's gaze steadily. "But we *will* be each other's lasts."

Saul nodded once. "You better be a switch, Jean-Paul."

Scoffing softly, Jean-Paul offered Saul a warm smile. "For you, *bien-aimé*, I will be."

Accepting that, Saul grinned. "Good."

Jean-Paul decided that was enough talking for a while. Returning to his ministrations, he focused on driving Saul out of his ever-loving mind. He wanted his beloved to recall the night he bonded their life threads for the rest of their lives.

To that end, Jean-Paul licked, nipped, and sucked his way across Saul's torso, then down the center groove to his abdominals. He kept his hands moving, massaging his way down his sides and over his hips. When Jean-Paul began mapping Saul's eight-pack with his tongue and lips, Saul's cock head bumped against his chin, and a groan erupted from his beloved.

"That's it," Jean-Paul encouraged, enjoying the sounds his

beloved made. "Love hearing what my touch does to you."

Scraping his thumbnail down the V-groove along his right hip, Jean-Paul teased what he knew was traditionally sensitive skin. He wasn't disappointed. His beloved sucked in a harsh breath, his abdominals trembling beneath his lips. When Jean-Paul rubbed through the hair of his groin, Saul sucked in a harsh gasp before whispering his name.

Jean-Paul smiled, reveling in that response. Working his way down, he nuzzled his cheek against Saul's thick weeping erection. He turned his head to kiss along his beloved's heated, swollen flesh. As he did that, he lowered his hand to gently cradle his beloved's balls.

"Oh, fuck! Jean-Paul," Saul cried, his hips shifting restlessly. "So good. What, ugh, please more."

Loving the sound of his name on Saul's lips, Jean-Paul smiled against his lover's erection. "I'll give you more," he crooned huskily. "I'll give you everything you need."

"Please," Saul gasped again.

Jean-Paul gave Saul what he assumed he wanted. Opening his mouth and turning his head, he wrapped his lips around his beloved's flesh. His senses sang, swamped by the taste, feel, and scent of the human who was the other half of his soul. The sensation caused his own cock to throb, and he knew he needed to move things forward before he did something crazy . . . like embarrass himself.

Can't remember the last time I was ever so on edge.

Grabbing the lube he'd set to the side, Jean-Paul quickly popped the cap. He released Saul's balls just long enough to pour a liberal amount of slick onto his fingers. Then he closed it and tossed it to the side. Utilizing centuries of skill, Jean-Paul easily found Saul's hole.

"Yeah," Saul grunted, rocking his hips. "Do it."

So Jean-Paul did. He slid his finger deep into his lover's rectum. Crooking his finger as he slowly withdrew it, he unerringly found Saul's prostate.

Saul's howl of pleasure filled the room, sending Jean-Paul's smug satisfaction soaring. Keeping his fingers moving—one becoming two, then three quickly enough—he continued massaging Saul's prick with his lips and tongue. Jean-Paul ended up moving the hand on Saul's balls to his hip when he began rocking beneath him, holding him in place.

"Jean-Paul!" Saul cried.

In the next instant, Jean-Paul felt his beloved's hands sink into his hair. He almost winced at the tight hold. Except, the flood of cream filling his mouth distracted him.

Jean-Paul groaned appreciatively as the exquisite flavor of Saul's cum burst across his taste buds. The slightly salty good-ness tasted almost as fantastic as his beloved's blood. While he hadn't blown too many men over the years, and none in the last century, Jean-Paul knew that sucking off his human would become one of his new favorite pastimes.

Delicious.

When Saul finally stopped spurting, Jean-Paul licked along his shaft, teasing him while making certain he hadn't missed a drop. Then he carefully eased off his lover's bobbing prick and peered up at Saul's face. Jean-Paul smiled with satisfac-tion upon taking in his beloved's heavy-lidded gaze and sated expression.

Exquisite.

"You taste amazing, *bien-aimé*," Jean-Paul rumbled as he began teasing at Saul's prostate again. He spread his fingers a little, testing his readiness. "And you'll feel even better."

As Jean-Paul eased his fingers free of Saul's chute, he made certain to rub along his prostate. He grinned when his be-loved groaned softly, and his human's prick bobbed, betray-ing his continued arousal. His lover's heady scent filled the room, flooding Jean-Paul with a driving need.

"You're mine now, Saul," Jean-Paul declared as he grabbed for the lube again. "All mine." He quickly slicked up his dick, his anticipation ramping up. "Finally."

"I'm yours, Jean-Paul," Saul rumbled, peering up at him with a heavy-lidded gaze and a loopy-looking smile. "That what you want to hear?"

Groaning, Jean-Paul lined himself up. "*Oui*," he confirmed gruffly. He met Saul's gaze, seeing the welcoming warmth within his blue eyes. Unable to help himself, Jean-Paul came as close as he'd come to begging . . . ever . . . when he asked, "Say it again."

Saul's smile widened. His big hands tightened on Jean-Paul's upper arms and urged him down. After pecking a hard kiss to Jean-Paul's lips, Saul eased away and met his gaze. His eyes were clear and expression warm as he stated, "Jean-Paul, I am yours."

Jean-Paul whispered Saul's name reverently before giving in to his basest of instincts. As he thrust, his hips surging forward, driving his prick deep inside his beloved's hot, willing body, he could think only one thing.

I will make him scream my name.

With single-minded determination, Jean-Paul rutted into Saul again and again. He pegged his beloved's prostate over and over, causing him to writhe with the pleasure he gave him. True to his vow, Jean-Paul reveled in Saul's moans and cries.

When Jean-Paul heard the sound of his name on his human's lips, he reached between them and gripped his lover's thick shaft. Two jacks had his lover's body bowing beneath him, his hand being coated in his seed.

Saul called Jean-Paul's name again, the exquisite cry filling him with a sense of rightness he'd never before experienced.

Jean-Paul rocked forward and struck, sinking his fangs deep into his beloved's flesh, claiming him for all time.

CHAPTER NINE

Saul stretched languidly, enjoying not only the extremely comfortable bed, but also the strong arms around him. After several rounds of sex the evening before, intermingled with quiet conversation, his chute was deliciously sore, and he wondered if he would be able to get it up for days. He had a funny feeling that if he told his bedmate that, Jean-Paul would take it as a personal challenge and start another round.

The vampire was damn insatiable.

And I loved every second of it.

"Good," Jean-Paul murmured huskily into his ear. "I did, too."

Right. That's another thing I'm still working on. Keeping my thoughts to myself.

One of the things Saul had learned the evening before was that bonded vampire couples could speak telepathically to each other. Evidently, he had loud thoughts, and everything he thought was being projected to Jean-Paul. His vampire lover had needed to show him how to mentally control his thoughts when he wanted to keep them to himself as well as how to will them to Jean-Paul when he wanted to share them.

Saul was still getting used to that. Fortunately, Jean-Paul didn't seem to mind when he shared something unintentionally. In fact, Jean-Paul had told him that he felt grateful to get a window into his random thoughts because it helped him learn about Saul faster.

As Saul felt Jean-Paul running an appreciative hand over his hip, he also felt his bladder twinge. With a groan, he turned and smiled at his lover.

Damn. Can't remember the last time I actually woke up with a guy.

Saul made certain that he kept that thought to himself. He knew his own jealousy when he thought of Jean-Paul with the donors at his coven was nothing compared to how territorial the vampire could be. While in post-coital bliss the evening before, Saul had made a comment about how he'd never imagined how being taken bare could feel, and he'd ruined him forever, and he would never want to go back to using condoms.

Jean-Paul had been quick to clutch Saul close, holding him in a proprietary gaze while saying, "You are mine, Saul. No one will ever get near you again, with condoms or not."

Rubbing his palms over Jean-Paul's sides, arms, and neck, Saul had soothed him, crooning, "I'm all yours, my vampire. You're all I'll ever want."

Fortunately, it had worked, and they'd relaxed together once more. Saul had asked about Jean-Paul's coven and the area where he lived. They'd chatted about that until Jean-Paul's roving hands had made their way to Saul's pubic hair, teasing the sensitive skin there, and they'd started another round.

Now, however, Saul gripped Jean-Paul's roving hand. "I'm sorry, Jean-Paul," he murmured apologetically as he met the vampire's questioning gaze. "I need to piss."

Jean-Paul hummed as he eased away from him. After a glance at the clock on the nightstand, which read ten-twenty-two, he also eased to a sitting position. "I suppose we've whiled away most of the morning." Cocking his head and narrowing his eyes, Jean-Paul mused, "And I hear Julian letting someone into the suite."

"You can hear through the walls?" Saul constantly found himself surprised by Jean-Paul's admissions. As he hurried to the bathroom, he added, "That's impressive."

"Thank you." Jean-Paul followed him, pausing at the shower and turning it on while Saul continued to the closed-off toilet room. Through the door, Saul heard Jean-Paul tell him, "Julian must have ordered breakfast. Let's hurry and get cleaned up before he eats it all."

Saul's growling stomach was more than on board with that idea.

While Saul couldn't remember the last time he'd gone commando, he didn't complain when he pulled on his jeans from the evening before. Jean-Paul offered him a clean shirt, but Saul couldn't imagine anything of the man's fitting him comfortably. He opted to go shirtless until he had to leave the suite. Saul kept his body in great shape, and he wasn't shy about it.

He'd tried to become a dancer, after all.

Saul followed Jean-Paul from the room, admiring his slacks-clad ass along the way. Evidently, the man hadn't brought any jeans. Absently, Saul wondered if the powerful man even owned any.

When Jean-Paul glanced behind him, Saul wondered if he'd accidentally broadcasted that thought. The vampire didn't say anything, though. Instead, he reached for Saul's hand and drew him closer . . . as if being a couple of feet apart was too far.

Going with it, not really minding, Saul allowed himself to be drawn toward the two trolleys laden with uncovered platters of food. He inhaled deeply, enjoying the aromas of the variety before him. Saul spotted cheesy scrambled eggs, bacon, sausage, pancakes, French toast, and some kind of hash brown casserole.

"Oh, wow." Saul hummed appreciatively. "That all looks amazing."

"Morning, Jean-Paul," Julian greeted, turning from where

he was pouring a cup of what smelled like coffee. "Morning, Saul. Can I offer you a cup?" He held up the carafe.

"Morning, and sure. Thanks," Saul replied with a nod.

"Yes, thank you, Julian," Jean-Paul answered. With a squeeze to Saul's hand, he asked, "How do you like your coffee?"

"If it's good coffee, black," Saul told him with a smirk. "And considering we're at the *Bellagio*, I bet it's good."

"This is my second cup, and it's decent for America," Julian told him, a teasing glint in his dark eyes.

Saul chuckled, not taking offense. "I suppose I'll try it black first, then." As he took a plate from Jean-Paul and began filling it with food, he glanced around. "Marty still asleep?" Smirking, he asked, "You wear my buddy out?"

Julian scoffed as he placed two cups of coffee on the round four-person table near the glass doors leading to the balcony. "No, Marty slipped out at a little after four this morning," Julian told him. "He thought I was asleep when he crept around the room, gathering his clothes, so I figured I'd let him go." Leaning against the table, Julian admitted, "While I would have been happy to have him stay for a morning round, I didn't know if stopping him would embarrass him or not."

Shaking his head, Saul told him, "If he was sneaking out, letting him go was probably the best course of action." Upon seeing Julian's concerned expression, Saul added, "I'll call him this afternoon to make sure he's all good."

"Thank you," Julian replied. "I know he's a one-night stand, but you mentioned he didn't normally do that with guys. He could be . . . in crisis?" His dark brows furrowed. "Is that the right word?"

Saul laughed softly as he carried his plate to the table. "So, stuff you did might have freaked him out a little, huh? TMI, man. TMI."

Julian scoffed softly, a smile toying around the corners of

his lips. As Saul settled in his chair, Jean-Paul to his right, Julian moved to the chair on Jean-Paul's other side. As the man eased onto the seat, his attention fell to Saul's neck.

His eyes widening a smidge, Julian snapped his gaze to Jean-Paul. "You claimed him," he murmured. After a glance at Saul, he refocused on Jean-Paul. "Does he know what that means?"

"Saul knows." Jean-Paul smiled as he reached over and rested his hand over Saul's wrist, since he had a fork in that hand. "We had many long conversations last night." With a leer, he added, "Between fun, of course." Then Jean-Paul turned his attention back to Julian. "He has accepted me, our nature, and has agreed to move to France with me."

Grinning broadly, Julian appeared truly happy for them. "Congratulations, Master Jean-Paul. It has been decades since the last beloved was found," he declared. "This will bring joy and hope to many members." With a wry smile, Julian added, "Myself included."

"Thank you, Julian." Jean-Paul smiled warmly at Saul. "Fate has truly blessed me."

As Saul used the side of his fork to cut into a piece of French toast, he returned Jean-Paul's smile. Still, a fissure of unease caused his gut to clench. These guys were so happy that Jean-Paul found Saul, his beloved.

Saul hoped he could live up to their expectations.

To Saul's relief, the pair fell silent. Jean-Paul focused on eating while Julian relaxed in a chair, sipped his coffee, and stared outside. For several minutes, there was little noise beyond the scrape of cutlery and the occasional appreciative hum as they ate or drank.

Just as Saul had thought, the coffee was excellent. He didn't know what brand the hotel offered, but he enjoyed it.

Saul finished the food on his plate and was contemplating getting seconds when there was a knock on the door.

Jean-Paul peered at Julian. "Are we expecting someone?" he asked as Julian rose to his feet.

Julian nodded. "Caspian, remember?"

"Ah, yes. Of course." Jean-Paul focused on Saul. "Caspian is the friend who I came here to visit. He and his husband have a couple of residences here in the States, but they were visiting here with a few friends and their husbands." He explained quickly, as Julian was headed to open the door. "Caspian and his friends are vampires, while their spouses are a mix of shifters and humans. From what I understand, Sebastian met his beloved, Dirk, here in Vegas at a Comicon. They're here celebrating their anniversary."

"Oh, wow," Saul murmured, his attention straying to the door as Julian opened it and greeted whoever was on the other side. "Is it wrong to ask the shifters about their animal?"

Saul had listened to Jean-Paul briefly touch on shifters the evening before. The idea of a person changing into a cognitive animal was fascinating to Saul. He could only imagine how interesting it would be to see the world from that perspective.

"As long as you know everyone in the room is aware of paranormals, these guys won't mind," Jean-Paul told him with a smile as he rose to his feet. "From what I understand, questioning some shifters can be hit or miss." Pointing at Saul's empty plate, he asked, "Do you want more?"

"I can wait," Saul stated, also rising.

Jean-Paul nodded, placing his hand on the small of Saul's back.

Sweeping his gaze over the group that had entered, Saul realized he would never have guessed that any of them were anything other than human. Who was paired with whom was easy to spot. Each pair were either holding hands or one had their arm around another.

Guess being touchy-feely is a paranormal thing.

Yes, we do love to touch our partners.

Hearing Jean-Paul's murmured words in his head, Saul

grimaced. *Sorry.*

You're fine, bien-aimé. Jean-Paul's voice held definite warmth. *You'll get it eventually.*

Locking down his thoughts, Saul focused on the people being introduced before him. The vampires were Caspian, Sebastian, Lexington, and Vince. They were bonded with Casey, Dirk, Nate, and Frankie.

Everyone offered Jean-Paul and Saul their congratulations. Frankie even welcomed him to the paranormal world, giving him a hug. Vince quickly pulled him back possessively, and Jean-Paul immediately wrapped his arm around Saul's waist. Frankie just laughed at their antics.

Nate offered Saul a reassuring smile as he told him, "I was lucky enough to have friends who already knew about vampires, so I had plenty of people who could answer my questions. If you need to talk, let me know." He indicated Dirk as he added, "We were both in your shoes not too long ago. We'd be happy to help clarify anything."

"Thanks, guys. I appreciate the offer." Saul did, too. He felt a little overwhelmed and a bit uncertain, even though he knew his decision to bond with Jean-Paul was the right choice. "I'll probably take you up on that."

Cocking his head, Dirk squinted at him. "You look really familiar to me. Have we met?"

Saul knew it wasn't a come-on, even though it sounded like a horrible pick-up line. Sweeping his gaze over the small man, he racked his brain. Unfortunately, he saw so many people in his line of work, he couldn't hope to recall many of them.

"Uh, sorry." Saul shrugged. "No idea."

"Saul was the host who showed us to our table on our first date," Sebastian stated, a smile curving his lips as he obviously recalled a fond memory. "Do you still work at *Emeril's*?"

"Yeah, I do," Saul confirmed, looking over them once more. He still couldn't place them, but he guessed they would have been there a few years back. "I still occasionally host as well as wait tables."

"We'll have to go there again," Dirk grinned up at Sebastian. "Is that okay?"

"Anything you want, my beloved," Sebastian replied before bending and pressing a kiss to Dirk's lips.

Yep, they're definitely touchy-feely.

Feeling Jean-Paul's arm around his waist, Saul decided he could definitely live with it.

CHAPTER TEN

U tilizing the SUV that Julian had rented for them, Jean-Paul drove them to the home where Saul lived. He'd been a little unnerved by the amount of jealousy that had surged through him when he'd first heard that his beloved was living with a single man named Daniel. Fortunately, Saul had been quick to assure him that they were just friends and had never been more than that.

Jean-Paul parked in the driveway and glanced around. The neighborhood appeared well-tended, and the homes were kept neat. Jean-Paul had never understood the allure of living in a cookie-cutter home, but he'd grown up in the days when nobles lived in large castles and it took days to ride to a neighbor.

Saul opening his door and sliding from the vehicle, drew Jean-Paul from his musings. Following his beloved, he strolled up the walk. From the corner of his eye, he saw Julian flanking him, the enforcer keeping watch.

After unlocking the front door, Saul entered, leading the way inside. "You guys want a drink or something while you wait?" he asked, heading through a front living room. "I'd like to shower and change, so it'll be a few."

While Saul had told Jean-Paul that he could have just dropped him off and he would meet him later, Jean-Paul had refused. It didn't matter that his beloved had assured him Reagan didn't know where Saul lived. His nature refused to allow his newly bonded beloved out of sight for any length of time.

Jean-Paul already knew that he would end up camped out at *Emeril's* bar the next day when Saul worked his shift.

"Water would be great," Julian replied. "It's hot out there."

Chuckling, Saul quipped, "Welcome to the desert."

"Same," Jean-Paul added. "Thank you, *bien-aimé*."

After Saul placed two bottles of water on the counter, he started out of the kitchen, saying, "I'll be as quick as I can."

Jean-Paul wrapped his arm around Saul's waist, stopping him. "Take as long as you need, *bien-aimé*. We are not in a hurry."

"Yeah, but you're on vacation," Saul countered, furrowing his brows. "There's plenty of sights to see while you're here."

Jean-Paul smiled up at his thoughtful human. "I'm going to sit at the table and extend my stay for a full two weeks, so I'll have plenty of time."

"Really? Why?"

Saul threaded his fingers through Jean-Paul's hair gently, and Jean-Paul appreciated that his lover was starting to grow comfortable with touching him back.

"If you put in your two-week notice at your work tomorrow, I intend on being here the entire time while you complete it."

Saul nibbled his bottom lip for a second before asking in a low voice, "Can you really be away from your coven that long?" He glanced toward Julian before refocusing on Jean-Paul. "I gotta apply for a visa to get into France anyway, and I have no idea how long that takes."

"You won't need a visa, *bien-aimé*," Jean-Paul countered with a wink. "I have a private jet and can easily smuggle you into the country." Upon seeing Saul's eyes widen in obvious surprise, he added, "Besides, we have to remake our identities many times over the centuries, so we're adept at forging information."

"Huh," Saul murmured. "That never occurred to me."

"Go shower and change, *bien-aimé*," Jean-Paul urged, lifting a hand to cradle the back of Saul's neck. "We will be fine here." Unable to help himself, he waggled his eyebrows and teased, "Unless you'd like some company in the shower?"

Saul chuckled and shook his head. "We already did that this morning, and I happen to know it took a really long time." Perhaps to soften his refusal, Saul told him, "This is just a quick rinse since I'm wearing the same clothes as yesterday."

Jean-Paul smiled. "Of course."

With a gentle tug to the back of Saul's neck, Jean-Paul urged his taller beloved to bend, allowing him to press a firm kiss to his lips. He licked at his beloved's bottom lip, and when Saul opened, he couldn't resist taking a quick taste. Knowing they could get out of hand fast, Jean-Paul drew back before that could happen.

"Go, *bien-aimé*," Jean-Paul urged again, lowering his hands and taking a step backward.

Saul nodded and turned, nearly running into a human who'd been rounding the corner. "Oh, sorry, Daniel." He indicated them, saying, "This is Jean-Paul and Julian. Guys, this is Daniel. I'll be back shortly."

"Daniel," Jean-Paul greeted, holding out his hand.

"Jean-Paul." After they shook, Daniel headed into the kitchen. "You French tourists in town for a few days?"

"Yes," Jean-Paul replied with a nod, picking up both bottles of water. He handed one to Julian. They settled at the table, making themselves comfortable.

Daniel grabbed his own bottle of water. As he unscrewed the cap, he leaned his hip against the counter and asked, "Saul showing you around while you're here?"

"He is," Jean-Paul confirmed.

"He stay with you guys last night?" Daniel continued to question him. He glanced between them. "Threesome?"

Jean-Paul smiled at the nosey human. "Yes, to him staying with me last night. No, to the threesome." He barely kept the growl out of his voice as he glanced Julian's way, who sported a slight smirk. "I will never share Saul," he continued, returning his attention to Daniel. "And he'll be staying with me for the duration of my stay, where I intend to woo him and convince him to run away with me."

Daniel set the bottle on the counter and frowned at him. "You just met last night, and you want to take him to France?" Then he narrowed his eyes and asked, "Or do you live in the States now?"

"We live in Montpellier, France." Jean-Paul saw no reason to hide the fact from the human. He was Saul's friend, after all. "You'll have to come visit him there once he's settled."

Staring, Daniel remained silent.

Hmmm . . . I think I shocked your friend. Jean-Paul reached out to Saul, figuring he should warn his beloved of what he'd shared with the man.

How'd you manage to do that?

Pleased that Saul was getting the hang of using their bond, Jean-Paul passed on what he'd told Daniel. *I told him I intend to woo you and take you away with me.*

He's always known me to be pretty level-headed. Saul's amusement came through even in his mental voice. *He'll definitely question me about it.*

I'll leave it to your discretion on what to say. Just know I won't be leaving here without you.

Saul's response was immediate. *I know.*

"Saul doesn't have any blood family, but he's like a little brother to me," Daniel slowly stated, redrawing Jean-Paul's attention. "So I'm gonna be the one to say it." He scowled at Jean-Paul while growling, "If you hurt him, I'll find a way to fly over the pond and kick your ass." Crossing his arms over his chest, Daniel added, "And I'm gonna let Saul know that I'll always be happy to buy him a plane ticket back here if things go sideways."

Instead of being offended, Jean-Paul smiled at Daniel. "It pleases me to know he has a friend like you to watch his back," he told the wary human. "And I'll respond with, there is no way I'll allow things to go sideways." Jean-Paul hesitated an instant, but he couldn't help but add, "Saul is the love of my life, and I've been searching for him for years."

"Love of your life?" Daniel scoffed. "You met him yesterday." Picking his water back up, he asked, "Is this a French thing?"

Shaking his head, Jean-Paul opened his own bottle of water. "It is something unique to my family line," he decided to go with. "We are all aware that when we meet *the one*" — he lifted his free hand and made air quotes — "we'll know it."

"Seriously?" Daniel didn't seem convinced.

Julian nodded, lifting his hand for attention. "I'm his cousin," he lied smoothly. "We've seen it happen many times over the years. We just know."

"That's weird," Daniel stated, obviously still skeptical. He seemed to let it go, however, taking a drink of his water before asking, "So, has Saul told you where he's taking you?"

"We're going to the *Luxor* to check out some of their attractions first," Julian told him, resting his forearms on the table and cradling his water between them. "For dinner, we're meeting up with friends and going to the Tournament of Kings dinner show at *Excalibur*."

"You're taking Saul to *Excalibur*'s Tournament of Kings dinner show?" Daniel sounded impressed. "He's talked about checking that out for years but never has."

Jean-Paul recalled the way Saul's eyes had lit up when they'd talked about it. He'd been a little worried he wouldn't be able to get an extra ticket on such short notice. Fortunately, the *Bellagio*'s concierge had managed it.

"I look forward to sharing it with him, then," Jean-Paul

stated. Deciding to see what else the man would share, he asked, "Do you know of any other things he's wanted to do but hasn't gotten around to yet?"

"Uh." Daniel paused, staring down at the counter with furrowed brows for so long that Jean-Paul wondered if he would be able to come up with anything. Finally, Daniel lifted his gaze back to him and told him, "You know about the attractions at the top of the *Stratosphere*?" After Jean-Paul nodded once—he'd heard something about them, although he didn't know specifics, something he would correct immediately—Daniel told him, "They put in a new one a couple of years ago. A type of free-fall drop off the side. He's mentioned a couple of times that he thought it would be cool."

Julian had his phone out and held it out to Jean-Paul. "This."

Reading the description, Jean-Paul felt his throat close. He exchanged a look with his enforcer, and he knew the other vampire was thinking the exact same thing. His beloved wanted to be strapped into a harness and dropped off the side of a building.

How the hell will I be able to watch my beloved do something so dangerous?

"Damn," Jean-Paul whispered before focusing on Daniel. "He really wants to try that?"

"Not a fan of heights?" Daniel smirked at him.

Jean-Paul scowled at him. "Not a fan of the man I'm falling for doing something that will put his life in jeopardy."

"It's perfectly safe," Daniel countered with a grin. "Hundreds of people do it every day." Chuckling, he added, "So, I shouldn't tell you about Saul's desire to learn how to hang glide?"

"What?" Jean-Paul would forever deny his gasp.

"Knock that shit off, man," Saul grumbled, appearing around the corner carrying a duffle bag over his left shoulder. "Stop freaking him out." Meeting Jean-Paul's gaze, Saul told him, "I have zero desire to learn how to hang glide."

Blowing out a breath of relief, Jean-Paul rose. "Good." He wrapped his arms around Saul's waist and peered up at him. "That would definitely give me premature gray hairs."

Saul laughed and shook his head. "Can't have that now, can we?"

"Let's not," Jean-Paul replied. After standing on his toes and pecking a kiss to Saul's lips, he took a step back, taking Saul's bag in the process. "Are we ready, then?"

"Yep." Saul turned toward Daniel. "You need anything before I leave for a few days?"

"You're really moving into his hotel room while he's here?" Daniel was clearly still in disbelief about that.

Saul grinned and waggled his brows. "Well, I'd invite him here, but I think listening to us shag would end up embarrassing the both of us."

Groaning, Daniel rolled his eyes. "Yep. TMI, man." He sobered, leveling a serious gaze upon him. "You sure about this, Saul?"

Nodding, Saul replied, "I'm sure." He lifted his arm, and they exchanged fist-bumps. "But thanks for worrying about me."

"He said he's going to try to convince you to move to France," Daniel blurted, frowning. "After knowing you one night."

With a shrug, Saul admitted, "I already told him I'd go."

"You what?" Daniel roared.

CHAPTER ELEVEN

"We'll be sorry to lose you," Ryan told him as he accepted Saul's two-week notice. "You've always been one hell of a worker." His soon-to-be former boss smiled at him as he asked, "Got big plans then?"

Saul nodded. "Moving to France with my boyfriend."

"Well, damn." Ryan grinned. "That *is* big plans. Good for you." Then he began leading Saul out of the office. "Is he that handsome fellow at the bar who eyed you like a steak your entire shift?"

Chuckling, Saul exited the room as he nodded. "Yeah. He's still in the possessive stage."

"As long as it's the kind of possessiveness you like."

Saul heard the warning in Ryan's voice. Between Daniel, Marty, and Ryan, he realized he had quite a few people who were worried for him. After admitting to Daniel that he had already accepted Jean-Paul's invitation, it had taken him ten minutes to get out of the house.

"It's definitely the best kind of possessiveness," Saul assured Ryan, smiling at the thought. "It feels really good, actually."

It did, too. While Saul didn't think he would feel that way with anyone else, considering the paranormal aspect of it, he realized he'd been missing out on life. He didn't think he would have been able to change anything, though.

Doesn't matter, anyway.

"Well, you have seniority," Ryan reminded him, patting him on the shoulder. "So if there's any shifts you need or don't want to take over the next couple of weeks, let me know."

"I appreciate that," Saul responded, meaning it. "But what I've been working is fine. I'll finish out my responsibilities."

"You're a good man, Saul," Ryan told him, starting in another direction. "I hope your man knows that."

"I do," Jean-Paul cut in as he approached. "I know it very well." After a smile and nod in Ryan's direction, he focused on Saul. "Are you ready, *bien-aimé*? Julian is bringing the car around, and I'm certain Nate and Dirk will be waiting for you."

Saul nodded. "Yep. I'm ready." He was having a meal with the human beloveds of Jean-Paul's vampire friends. After a couple of days with Jean-Paul, Saul was ready to talk to humans in the same situation as himself. It was time he learned what to expect from the human's point of view. "I appreciate you letting me do this."

Jean-Paul rested his hand on Saul's back as he guided him through the casino. "My beloved," he crooned. "You never need permission to do anything." Holding Saul's gaze, Jean-Paul told him, "I just need to know where you are and with whom, so I know you'll be safe."

"I get it," Saul assured, smiling at his lover. "I really do."

Saul did get it. Vampires were protective in a way Saul had never experienced before. He was still getting used to it.

Thirty minutes later, after battling the usual heavy traffic, Saul and the guys eased from the parked vehicle. He hesitated only an instant before reaching out and threading his fingers with Jean-Paul's. His vampire lover squeezed his hand as he gave him a smile that caused Saul's heart to skip a beat.

God, is that what love looks like?

Fortunately, Saul didn't get a response from Jean-Paul, telling him that he'd managed to keep the errant thought to himself.

Julian grabbed the door and held it open. Once in the foyer, Jean-Paul grabbed the next one. Instead of allowing Saul to enter, he tugged him to a stop. It was only after Julian quickly moved around him, entering first, that Jean-Paul allowed Saul to continue.

"Paranoid much?" Saul teased, amusement filling him.

"With your safety? Always," Jean-Paul replied seriously.

Saul felt his stomach warm as butterflies bumped within.

Julian pointed off to the left. "There's Nate and Dirk." Then he used a thumb to point the other way. "And it looks like the rest of the guys are over there." With a chuckle, Julian murmured, "Guess the guys were serious about giving the three of you space to chat." With a wink, he added, "Just not too much space."

Saul chuckled, too, as Jean-Paul guided him in that direction. Once they reached the table where Nate and Dirk were sitting, drinks already before them, Jean-Paul tugged him down for a quick kiss. Even as Saul felt his cheeks heat at the public display, he would never deny his lover.

"Enjoy your dinner, *bien-aimé*," Jean-Paul encouraged, pulling out Saul's chair for him. "You know where I'll be if you need anything."

Nodding, Saul took the seat. "Thanks."

After giving greetings to the other men, Jean-Paul headed away. Saul couldn't help but watch him go, his attention riveted on the man's ass. The slacks cradled his butt to perfection, and Saul felt his fingers twitch with his desire to squeeze the globes.

"I know exactly what you're thinking," Nate teased, cradling his beer between his palms. "And it's totally normal."

"And I bet it doesn't ever go away," Dirk piped up, pushing his thick red hair out of his eyes. "It's part of the bond."

Saul tore his gaze away from Jean-Paul only after he'd sat at the table with the other paranormals. Glancing between the pair, seeing they wore identical understanding looks, he let out a deep breath. He opened his mouth, intending to ask how long they'd been with their vampires, but the arrival of the waitress stopped him.

After a quick glance at the menu, Saul gave the woman his order of beer and a burger.

"So." Nate leaned forward, resting his elbows on the table. "What's troubling you, big man?"

Hearing the teasing in Nate's tone, Saul relaxed. He smiled and mirrored the guy's pose. Dirk did the same, allowing them to talk quietly in the busy restaurant.

"What if I do something that will make Jean-Paul's people think less of him?" Saul asked softly, frowning at his hands. "I mean, he's their leader. I'm a waiter. I suck at learning languages, and now I'm moving to France." His gut churned as he thought about how badly he could screw up. "That's a whole different culture." Glancing between Nate and Dirk, Saul admitted, "What if I make some *faux pa* without evening knowing?"

Nate reached over and patted Saul's hand. "Trust me," he began. "There's nothing you could do that would ever reflect badly on your man." With a quiet laugh, Nate told him, "You could spill your salad on a visiting dignitary and Jean-Paul would be asking you if you were okay instead of worrying about the dignitary."

"Really?" While Saul couldn't imagine actually doing that, he thought it strange. "But—"

The waitress arrived with Saul's beer. "Here you are, sir." She smiled a flirty smile as she told him, "Your meals should be out soon. Is there anything else I can get you in the meantime?"

Saul figured she'd missed Jean-Paul kissing and seating him. While he'd found women attractive in the past, he realized she did absolutely nothing for him. In fact, he was more annoyed that she was hitting on him than anything else.

"No, I'm good." Dismissing her, Saul looked to the other guys. "You guys want anything?"

Nate looked like he was fighting a laugh. Shaking his head, he looked to Dirk. The redhead probably missed the interaction, for he tapped his glass and stated, "I'll take a refill, please."

The woman confirmed the type of wine Dirk was drinking before heading away. When she glanced over her shoulder at him, Saul ignored her.

"You probably get that a lot," Nate teased, letting out his amused chuckle.

"Get what a lot?" Dirk asked, glancing between them.

Nate pointed at Saul. "The waitress was totally eyeing him up."

"Huh." Dirk shrugged. "Okay. Anyway." Just that fast, he returned the subject to their discussion. "So, you're the most important person in Jean-Paul's life now. Your happiness is his biggest priority."

"As well as your safety." Nate picked up the explanation. "So no doing dangerous stuff."

Saul nodded. "Yeah, I caught onto that one." With a roll of his eyes, he explained Daniel's shenanigans. "When I walked in, it looked like Jean-Paul had lost three shades."

"Ouch. That was mean." Dirk winced. "Glad you really don't want to do that stuff."

"Definitely not," Saul confirmed. "I like having both my feet on the ground." After taking a gulp of his beer, appreciating the hoppy flavor, he felt his bladder twinge. "Okay. Gonna hit the head before our food arrives." Saul stood and glanced around, looking for the men's room sign. Spotting it to the left, he told the guys, "Be right back."

Saul strode toward the side of the restaurant. Before entering the side hall, he glanced to the right. He spotted Jean-Paul watching him and smiled at his vampire. When Saul received a warm smile back, he felt his nerves ease.

As Saul pissed into a urinal, he thought about that look. With that one expression, his vampire had proved his watchfulness and fondness. Maybe that was all there was to it.

I'm his beloved, and that means everything to him.

No matter what, Jean-Paul would be on his side.

Saul smiled as he shook off and zipped up. He'd just finished washing his hands when the men's room door opened. Glancing behind him, already turning to grab a paper towel, Saul froze.

"Reagan."

The man sneered. "Told you I'd catch up with you without your Frenchies out there."

Before Saul could react, one of Reagan's henchmen slammed the butt of a gun against Saul's temple, and it was lights out.

Saul's groggy mind slowly moved toward consciousness. Pain radiated through his right temple, making thinking sluggish. He blinked a couple of times, but all he saw was darkness. When Saul attempted to lift his right hand, intending to rub at his eyes, he couldn't move it.

Sucking in a sharp breath, Saul realized several things at once. First, he was having trouble breathing and seeing because there was something covering his head. Second, he was tied up. Third, he recalled Reagan catching up with him in the restaurant's bathroom.

Oh, shit.

Saul? Answer me, damn it. Jean-Paul's urgent cry echoed through his already pain-filled mind. That was followed up by a string of French that Saul didn't understand.

Jean-Paul? When Saul mentally called his vampire's name, his lover's ranting ceased. *Reagan caught me in the restaurant bathroom. I just woke up.*

Where did Reagan take you? Jean-Paul sounded angry, even in Saul's mind. *I will tear him limb from limb . . . very slowly.*

As much as Saul didn't want to admit it, it wasn't as if he could hide the fact. *Uh, not sure. There's a bag over my head, and I'm tied to a chair.*

Even as Saul finished sending his thought to Jean-Paul, the bag was whisked from his head. He blinked quickly, struggling to get his eyes to focus. Saul's gut rolled when he saw Luigi Arnasta, the crime boss himself, sitting behind a large desk positioned in front of him.

"Ah, you're awake. Good," Luigi stated unnecessarily. His smile appeared cold and sinister. "Reagan here tells me that you've been ignoring his calls and avoiding him."

The heavy-set black man flicked one finger to the right, and Saul saw Reagan leaning against the wall. The bag that had been on Saul's head dangled between two fingers. A sneer of distaste twisted his lips.

"That was not a wise decision, Saul," Luigi stated, redrawing Saul's attention. "After you get a lesson to refresh your memory about obeying us, I'll explain why I once again need your special services." Luigi leaned back in his chair and focused on Reagan. "Remember, don't break anything. He'll need his limbs intact to drive the car."

Oh, shit.

Saul? What's going on? Once again, Jean-Paul's voice came to him. *Do you know where you are?*

Saul realized that, while he might be alone, he wasn't on his own. Watching Reagan push away from the wall and begin stalking toward him, he told his vampire where he was pretty certain he was being held. After all, while Luigi Arnasta was a crime boss that the cops could never seem to pin anything on, he was also a businessman.

Reagan had brought Saul to Luigi's office building.

CHAPTER TWELVE

"I know where he is," Jean-Paul declared, quickly typing the address into the SUV's GPS system. "We need to hurry."

Julian replied by pressing harder on the gas, making the vehicle surge forward.

Jean-Paul glanced behind him and saw that the vehicle containing Caspian, Lexington, Vince, and Frankie was following closely. After discovering Saul missing from the men's room, Sebastian had taken Casey, Nate, and Dirk to their hotel. While Jean-Paul had assured an apologetic Nate and Dirk that it wasn't their fault, Jean-Paul did blame himself. He'd known his beloved was wanted by the city's seedy underbelly, but he hadn't followed him into the men's room.

That had been almost thirty minutes before, and Jean-Paul had mentally screamed Saul's name damn near every second of it. Finally, *finally*, his beloved had responded. Jean-Paul intended to make Reagan pay tenfold for every hurt he'd inflicted on Saul.

"We'll get him back," Julian finally stated, probably trying to reassure him. "We're almost there."

Except, the only thing that would reassure Jean-Paul was having Saul back in his arms.

Julian turned off the road and parked in the fire lane before an office building. Jean-Paul was out the door and racing toward the front doors. Only the rule of never revealing vampires to the public kept him from using his vampiric speed.

Jean-Paul could sense others behind him, and he knew his friends kept pace.

"Do you know what suite holds Luigi's office?" Julian asked, moving past Jean-Paul just in time to open the door for him.

"No, and Saul doesn't know," Jean-Paul admitted. He spotted the information board in the lobby, but the security guard behind the desk on the left offered a better option. "Come on."

Jean-Paul stalked toward the man, hazing his eyes as he moved. "Tell me where Luigi's office is," he demanded, barely keeping his talons sheathed.

The security guard's face went slack, and he turned to his computer. "Luigi who?"

"Luigi Arnasta," Jean-Paul snapped, barely controlling his impatience.

The guard tapped on the computer for a moment, setting Jean-Paul's teeth on edge. Finally, the man stated, "Luigi Arnasta is on floor thirty-two, corner office suite B-1800."

The guard had barely gotten the final words out of his mouth when Jean-Paul spun and raced toward the stairs. The elevator would take too long. He nearly yanked the door off its hinges in his haste to enter the stairwell.

"Wait, who are you?" the guard called, having woken from Jean-Paul's trance. "Visitors have to check in."

Ignoring the human, Jean-Paul streaked up the stairs, his feet barely touching the steps as he almost flew up them. He reached the thirty-second floor in seconds. Except, Jean-Paul found the door locked, and there was a card-swipe machine on the wall.

"Screw that," Vince muttered from behind him. Lifting his booted foot, he slammed it into the door near the lock. The molding splintered, metal screeched, and wood shattered, spraying across the hall floor, revealed by the swinging door.

Jean-Paul grunted his thanks as he glanced around, trying to get his bearings.

Where the hell would Suite B-1800 be?

The dull thud of flesh hitting flesh drew Jean-Paul's attention, and an angry snarl erupted from his throat. He sprinted toward the sound, fearing the worst. Jean-Paul hated to think just how roughed up his sweet beloved could have become on their race across town.

Spotting the closed suite door ahead, Jean-Paul barely registered the half dozen humans loitering in the lobby. His friends engaged them, leaving him free to break down the door, completely bypassing the knob. The door slammed into the wall and started back toward him, and Jean-Paul held up an arm to stop it.

Seeing Saul tied to a chair with Reagan standing over him, Jean-Paul saw red. He lunged forward, grabbed the human by the throat, and flung him across the room. Jean-Paul grew his claws, slicing through Saul's bonds.

"Who the hell are you?" the man behind the desk roared as he rose to his feet. He yanked open a drawer and withdrew a gun. "Hold it right there."

Jean-Paul stepped in front of Saul, blocking him from possible harm. Hazing his eyes, he pushed his will into the man's mind — Luigi Arnasta. He saw the depravity Luigi's actions had wrought — drugs, guns, and human trafficking. Evidently, the homeless were a prime target for his people, and he'd intended for Saul to drive a transport truck, just in case they ran into trouble.

Huh. My beloved is an exceptional driver.

Dismissing that for later contemplation, Jean-Paul ordered, "You will turn yourself into the police, Luigi."

"I will turn myself into the police," Luigi repeated, lowering the gun.

"You will tell them everything, unraveling your entire operation as well as every contact you have."

Once again, Luigi repeated him.

"You will leave and do it right now."

"I will do it now." Luigi placed the gun on his desk and

started walking toward the door.

Turning, Jean-Paul watched Luigi go.

"This's all your fucking fault," Reagan roared, having risen to his knees. He'd pulled a gun from somewhere and fired.

Jean-Paul grabbed Saul and spun. Feeling the impact of each bullet, he grunted. He heard Saul cry his name, but his tongue stuck in his mouth as pain surged through him.

When Jean-Paul heard the click-click, indicating the weapon was empty, he turned and growled low in his throat as he swallowed hard. "You, on the other hand," he rumbled, stalking toward the clearly shocked human. "You, I am going to kill."

"Jean-Paul?" Saul whispered his name.

Without pulling his attention away from Reagan, Jean-Paul ordered, "Look away, *bien-aimé*."

Jean-Paul saw Reagan reaching into his jacket and pulling out another clip. Lunging forward, he swung his arm. He slashed his talons across Reagan's throat, severing his carotid.

Instantly, Reagan dropped the gun and clip to grab at his throat.

Taking a step backward, Jean-Paul peered into Reagan's eyes, watching him bleed out. "You were warned," he rumbled, not feeling the least bit guilty.

Slowly, the light from Reagan's blue eyes faded, and he dropped unceremoniously to the floor.

Pulling a handkerchief from the inside of his suit coat, Jean-Paul wiped his talons. As he retracted them, he turned to find Saul staring at the far wall. Jean-Paul crossed to his beloved and rested his hand on his shoulder, gaining his attention.

The only thing that kept Jean-Paul from wrapping his big beloved in his arms was the fact that he didn't know where he might be hurting.

"Saul, are you okay?" Jean-Paul asked softly.

Saul turned, revealing wide blue eyes filled with worry.

"You were shot over half a dozen times," he murmured, his voice sounding strained. "How are you still standing?"

"Increased strength and healing, *bien-aimé*," Jean-Paul softly reminded his beloved. "I will heal swiftly enough as long as the bullets are removed."

"You got shot?" Julian snarled, stalking into the room. "Blaise will have my hide that you were injured."

"Who's Blaise?" Saul asked, scowling.

"My coven second," Jean-Paul told him, ignoring Julian's ire. "Now, please, Saul." He rested his palms on Saul's pectorals lightly. "We heard Reagan strike you. Where are you injured?"

Saul reached down and lifted his shirt, revealing his ripped abdominals. "Reagan liked to talk, so that was the only hit he got in before you stopped him," he told him. Patting his stomach, Saul claimed, "Dude hit like a girl."

"Better not let Camille hear you say something like that," Julian stated, although he sounded as if he was teasing.

"Who's that?" Saul asked.

Jean-Paul realized he still had plenty of things to explain to his beloved. "She is one of my enforcers," he told him.

"Let me see where you were shot," Julian demanded, frowning at him. "We can't leave any blood here, so I'll need to collect the slugs."

Sighing, Jean-Paul knew Julian was right. With slow movements, he carefully eased out of his suit jacket. Then he turned his back to Julian, letting him see what he knew would be a blood-soaked blue shirt.

"Good grief," Julian muttered as Saul sucked in a sharp breath. "Don't worry, Saul," his friend assured as he carefully eased the shirt up. "This will heal in no time." With a reassuring smile, Julian urged, "Why don't you let Jean-Paul hold you while I pop these out? It'll make him feel better."

Saul didn't appear convinced, but he rested his hands on

Jean-Paul's hips when he wrapped his beloved in his arms.

For the next few minutes, Jean-Paul focused on Saul, holding him in his arms, petting his torso and back, and inhaling his scent. He felt the occasional bite of pain as Julian popped the bullets from his body. Jean-Paul noticed the others enter, and Caspian assisted Julian in removing the slugs. Lexington used someone's shirt to make certain none of his blood dripped on the floor. Once they were done, Frankie and Vince quickly bandaged each healing hole.

"There," Julian muttered, wrapping the bullets in another bit of cloth. "Done. Now let's get out of here."

"Here."

Caspian offered Jean-Paul his suit jacket, which he took gratefully. With Saul's help, he eased it on, hiding the fresh bandages.

"Let's get you to your hotel room," Julian urged as he bundled everything in yet another shirt taken from another of the downed guards. "You can clean up, feed from Saul, and heal more swiftly."

"There's one thing that I need to do first," Jean-Paul countered as he allowed his clearly concerned Saul to guide him from the room.

"What's that?" Saul asked, worry furrowing his brows.

Almost thirty minutes later, Jean-Paul, Saul, and a slightly annoyed Julian stood before the *Bellagio* fountain.

With his arm wrapped around Saul's waist, Jean-Paul watched the fountains spray and dance to the music. He found Saul's expression of contentment even more mesmerizing than the display. Jean-Paul made a mental note to have something similar installed on the grounds of the coven estate.

Saul leaned down and whispered, "Thank you for bringing me to watch this with you, even though I think you're nuts for doing it after having bullets dug out of your back."

Jean-Paul chuckled softly upon hearing Saul's words. "When will you realize, *bien-aimé*? Pleasing you is more important than anything else in the world."

"It'll take some getting used to," Saul admitted, meeting his gaze with his warm blue eyes.

Returning his handsome beloved's smile, Jean-Paul murmured, "Good thing we have all the time in the world."

Saul nodded before bending and pecking a kiss to Jean-Paul's lips before returning his attention to the show.

Jean-Paul pressed into Saul's side, enjoying the show and his beloved's happy, contented scent.

ABOUT THE AUTHOR

Charlie started writing fantasy when she was eight, and after stumbling onto her first erotic romance at age nineteen, she realized her true calling. She now focuses on writing gay erotic romance, normally of the paranormal variety, with heroes of all kinds. With the help and support of her husband, Charlie finally fulfilled one of her life-long goals . . . move to acreage with her horses. You can often find her curled up with her laptop and a cup of tea or glass of wine, creating her next adventure. Charlie enjoys exploring the mountains of her new Oregon home on horseback, 4-wheeler, or motorcycle.

She can be reached at ch.richards2010@yahoo.com
Or visit her at www.charlie-richards.com.

www.ingramcontent.com/pod-product-compliance
Lightning Source LLC
Chambersburg PA
CBHW070529130626
46555CB00003B/1338